New dangers. New enemies. New adventures.

## SHARDS OF ALDERAAN

While visiting the remains of their mother's home, Jacen and Jaina encounter a long-lost enemy of the Solo family . . .

## DIVERSITY ALLIANCE

Everyone is searching for Bornan Thul, but the young Jedi Knights may be too late—for their true enemy is about to show his shockingly familiar face . . .

## DELUSIONS OF GRANDEUR

As the search for Raynar Thul's father continues, the young Jedi Knights turn for help to a most unusual—and dangerous—source: the reprogrammed assassin droid, IG-88!

## JEDI BOUNTY

Lowbacca has gone to the planet Ryloth to investigate the Diversity Alliance. And the other young Jedi Knights have discovered one truth about the Alliance—you either join, or you die.

## THE EMPEROR'S PLAGUE

It's a race against time: the young Jedi Knights must find and destroy the Emperor's plague before it can be released. But they first must face Nolaa Tarkona. And her very lethal hired hand, Boba Fett.

*continued . . .*

And don't miss the thrilling "Rise of the Shadow Academy" cycle of Young Jedi Knight novels . . .

# HEIRS OF THE FORCE

The *New York Times* bestselling debut of the young Jedi Knights! Their training begins . . .

# SHADOW ACADEMY

The dark side of the Force has a new training ground: the Shadow Academy!

# THE LOST ONES

An old friend of the twins could be the perfect candidate for the Shadow Academy!

# LIGHTSABERS

At last, the time has come for the young Jedi Knights to build their weapons . . .

# DARKEST KNIGHT

The Dark Jedi student Zekk must face his old friends Jacen and Jaina—once and for all.

# JEDI UNDER SIEGE

The final battle between Luke Skywalker's Jedi academy and the evil Shadow Academy . . .

# STAR
## YOUNG JEDI KNIGHTS
# WARS.
### RETURN TO ORD MANTELL

# KEVIN J. ANDERSON
## and REBECCA MOESTA

BERKLEY JAM BOOKS, NEW YORK

STAR WARS: YOUNG JEDI KNIGHTS:
RETURN TO ORD MANTELL

A Berkley Jam Book / published by arrangement with
Lucasfilm Ltd.

PRINTING HISTORY
Berkley Jam edition / May 1998

All rights reserved.
®, ™ & © 1998 by Lucasfilm Ltd.
Material excerpted from *Trouble on Cloud City* © 1998 by Lucasfilm Ltd.
This book may not be reproduced in whole or in part,
by mimeograph or any other means, without permission.
For information address: The Berkley Publishing Group,
a member of Penguin Putnam Inc.,
200 Madison Avenue, New York, New York 10016.

The Penguin Putnam Inc. World Wide Web site address is
http://www.penguinputnam.com

Check out the Ace Science Fiction/Fantasy
newsletter, and much more, at Club PPI!

ISBN: 0-425-16362-8

BERKLEY JAM BOOKS®
Berkley Jam Books are published by The Berkley Publishing Group,
a member of Penguin Putnam Inc.,
200 Madison Avenue, New York, New York 10016.
BERKLEY JAM and its logo are trademarks
belonging to Berkley Publishing Corporation.

PRINTED IN THE UNITED STATES OF AMERICA

10  9  8  7  6  5  4  3  2  1

*To Angela M. Kato, whose hard work and charming personality helped us to find more time to write*

# acknowledgments

Special thanks to Sue Rostoni, Allan Kausch, and Lucy Autrey Wilson at Lucasfilm Licensing for their valuable input on this new story arc; Ginjer Buchanan and Jessica Faust at Berkley for putting their full support behind this series; the Star Wars fans at Dragon*Con's Matters of the Force panels for their enthusiastic brainstorming; Dave Dorman for his marvelous cover art; Dan Wallace and Rich Handley for their research and resource materials; the work of Brian Daley, Al Williamson, and Archie Goodwin for providing fodder for our imaginations; Catherine Ulatowski, Sarah Jones, and Angela Kato at WordFire, Inc., for keeping everything running smoothly; and Jonathan Cowan for being our first test-reader.

# 1

THE TREE STOOD in the middle of a small jungle clearing, its gnarled, woody tentacles writhing through the air in search of prey.

As Zekk approached, the tentacles twitched, sensing his movement. The sinuous vines were camouflaged, deceptively lush and green. He took another step forward. The ground around the tree's warty trunk was littered with bones—broken grayish-white remnants of previous victims, stripped of flesh, now decaying in the humid air of Yavin 4.

Zekk moved even closer, and the hungry tree trembled in anticipation. He told himself he had nothing to fear. Of course he would have been much more comfortable had he been carrying a lightsaber, a Jedi weapon that could counter any attack from this plant-thing—but that would have been too easy. Much too easy.

Zekk wasn't interested in a simple end to this exercise.

Instead, he carried only a plain staff. He had found the length of dried wood in the jungle and stripped off its bark. It was all the weapon he would allow himself to use in this important test.

He stepped forward, faced the writhing tentacle tree, and prepared to do battle. "I will let the Force guide me," he murmured to himself, "allow it to direct my Jedi reflexes to respond to any tricks the enemy may devise."

The carnivorous tentacle tree reached toward him, its deadly branches whispering together in a leafy sigh.

"Most of all," he went on in a hushed voice, "I must not let myself be tempted by the easy power I can unleash through the dark side." Zekk had already traveled the dark paths of the Force when he trained at the Shadow Academy. Now he was a new student learning to use the light side—but at the same time, he was an old student . . . with many scars on his conscience.

He raised his stick. The tree's tentacles quivered as it prepared for this easy prey.

"The Force is with me," Zekk said, and stepped in among the dangling branches, his staff held high.

Three of the whipping vines thrashed at him, making the stick their primary target. Zekk snapped his wrist downward. A loud *crack* rang out as the staff beat back two of the tentacles.

Another serpentine appendage crackled and

wrapped itself around Zekk's right wrist. Without hesitation, he tossed the staff to his left hand, swung it up, and battered the offending tentacle as he yanked his hand free.

His skin burned and tingled as the clutching vine tore away from his wrist. He realized then that this plant-thing exuded some kind of irritating acid through its tiny spines. His hand began to swell, but Zekk turned his concentration back to the vines that still lashed at him. He could deal with the pain later.

He struck left and right, knocking the thrashing vines away. His hand turned red and throbbed; he could barely bend his fingers. A forest of tentacles now whipped and clawed at him. He could have severed them all with a single sweep of a lightsaber blade, but Zekk drove them back one-handed, using only his staff.

Simple victories were not worth fighting for. Without a challenge, victory was meaningless. He had come here to learn a new lesson—and unlearn an old one.

To begin Zekk's training in the light side of the Force, Master Skywalker had told him to start with simple exercises to test his most basic skills. Somehow, Zekk didn't think that venturing out into the jungles to battle this carnivorous tree was quite what the Jedi teacher had in mind. Perspiration trickled down Zekk's face and neck. His long dark hair clung in damp strands around his emerald-green eyes.

Zekk smiled.

He gritted his teeth and drove inward. He had fought many times before. The Dark Jedi Brakiss had trained Zekk to become the Second Imperium's darkest knight. Together, they—along with many other followers of the Emperor's ways—had battled Luke Skywalker's students at the Jedi academy.

But Zekk and the other Dark Jedi had been soundly defeated, and Brakiss killed. Broken, Zekk had turned away from the dark side. Even though he had formerly been a close friend of the Solo twins, Jacen and Jaina, Zekk could not easily grant himself forgiveness. He couldn't just join his friends and begin training as a Jedi of the light side as if nothing had happened.

Instead, Zekk had gone off on his own to search for meaning in his life. He trained to become a bounty hunter and used his Jedi prowess to hunt down difficult bounties that no one else could capture. But in those months Zekk had learned something important about himself: although he had the skills, he didn't have the mind-set that would allow him to find *any* quarry for whatever reason and simply turn the victim over to anyone who happened to pay the price.

When Nolaa Tarkona, head of a subversive political group called the Diversity Alliance, had set an open bounty on the merchant Bornan Thul, Zekk had at first gone on the search, hoping to prove himself to Boba Fett and all the other bounty hunters. But Zekk had realized in time that the information Nolaa Tarkona wanted from the human merchant concerned a deadly human-killing plague—and that if he succeeded in his task, the entire human race might become extinct.

Such consequences had forced him to change his mind and join forces with the young Jedi Knights after all. After they defeated the Diversity Alliance and the Emperor's plague was destroyed, Zekk had decided to start all over again, to become a true Jedi Knight. This time he would do his training in the right way.

If only this tree would let him.

Shorter, spikier tentacles emerged from the bole of the tree, thrashing, grasping at him, but again Zekk drove them back with his staff. He could have pulled back at any time, but instead he pushed closer. Then, although the irritant chemical in his swollen right hand bothered him, he gripped the stick with both hands again. He would not let the pain slow him down.

Zekk didn't have any clear idea of how he would define "victory." He did not intend to kill the tree, but as his battle fever picked up, he fought more furiously, pounding the tentacles with his hard staff.

Another whiplike vine snapped sharply and struck him in the forehead just above his eye, drawing a trickle of blood. He reeled backward, blinking his eyes against the stinging tears and red droplets.

Suddenly, unexpectedly, two of the vines wrapped themselves around his stick, twisted hard, and yanked it from Zekk's hand, tearing the flesh on his palms. Then, as if sensing victory, the relentless tentacles also grabbed at his arms and legs. Zekk stood trapped in a blizzard of grasping strands.

A black static of anger overpowered his fear. Zekk used the Force to reach out and locate his stolen staff. He jerked the stick back toward him— so furiously that two vines ripped away from the central mass of the tree and began oozing clear sap.

With the dying tentacles still dangling from his staff, Zekk swung around, using it as a flail against the others. He used the Force again to tie several of the strands into knots and laughed out loud at how easy this battle was becoming.

Then, in a flash of comprehension, Zekk realized that he was not truly succeeding; he had unleashed his *anger* and tapped the dark side as a conduit to his Jedi skills.

"No!" he said through gritted teeth. He refused to win against the plant-thing in this way. Zekk threw the retrieved staff aside and stood unarmed as the stinging tentacles drew back, then poised themselves to attack with renewed force.

But Zekk kept his mind clear, his thoughts calm. "I am not your prey," he murmured.

The tree had no intelligence, just a rudimentary mass of vascular plant fiber with reflexes that responded like muscles. Hungry tentacles lashed at him—only to slide harmlessly away, as if his entire body were coated with some invisible super lubricant.

"I am not your prey," Zekk repeated.

The ineffective vines reached toward him, but they could not touch his skin. Sinuous appendages danced in frustration around his arms, his head, his back.

Zekk turned away from the tree and walked slowly beyond the reach of the grasping tentacles. He knew he had temporarily let down his guard, a failure of sorts. But he had seen the dark side, recognized it, and rejected it! He would put it behind him now. He felt as if he had emerged from a raging storm with only a few drops of water clinging to him. The storm was past. A sense of warmth and peace came over him.

At the edge of the clearing, standing beside the thick bushes, he saw Master Luke Skywalker watching him with a quiet smile on his face. "I'm proud of you, Zekk," he said. "It took courage to turn away from your old instincts. Sometimes it's harder to *unlearn* bad teaching than it is to learn new skills. It will be hard to forget what Brakiss taught you."

"Yes," Zekk said. "I've got to learn it the right way now. I feel like a kid learning to walk again—

and I thought I already knew how. It's . . . intimidating." He said the word in a small voice, as if reluctant to admit it. "All the tests and exercises here remind me of what I learned at the Shadow Academy. I'm afraid to do things the same way. I mean, what if I do them wrong again?"

"There's no single way to become a Jedi," Luke Skywalker said. "If it makes you more comfortable, we'll find a different path. Try a new assignment. Take something you're already good at—something you enjoy—and use the Force, little by little, to enhance your abilities. It doesn't have to be fighting with a staff, or levitating rocks, or sensing danger. The Force is in all things. Find a task that feels right. Enjoy it, but let the Force guide you. You need to learn to accept your Jedi abilities, not fear them."

"I can try anything?" Zekk said. "Anything I enjoy?"

"I'm sure you can think of something, Zekk," Luke said.

The dark-haired young man just smiled.

Jedi trainees dragged a few more dried branches and pieces of dead wood from the surrounding jungle and piled it high in the courtyard. Master Luke Skywalker readied a bonfire while his students gathered to hear him speak.

Jacen Solo ran a hand through his tousled hair, scratched an itch on his scalp, and settled down on the ledge beside his friend Tenel Ka. They had found seats on one of the stone blocks of the rebuilt pyramid's lower levels; from there they would have a good view of the fire and Jacen's uncle Luke.

Jacen's twin sister Jaina, who loved to tinker with machines, had spent the afternoon with their Wookiee friend Lowbacca and his miniaturized translating droid, Em Teedee. They had worked beneath the Hapan passenger cruiser's navigational consoles, upgrading its starmaps and position-finding capabilities. As Princess of Hapes, the warrior girl Tenel Ka actually owned the *Rock Dragon,* but she preferred to let Jaina and Lowie pilot it.

Now the two tinkerers and the tiny, silver droid hurried up to sit beside Jacen and Tenel Ka as four new students prepared to light the bonfire.

Jaina still had a few smudges of grease on her cheeks and chin. Lowie's ginger-colored fur was ruffled, but they both looked satisfied.

"So, the ship's up and working again?" Jacen asked. "There's no telling when we might need to grab it and go rescue somebody. We're Jedi Knights now, you know."

Jaina gave an unladylike snort, as if insulted at the suggestion that she might not have left the ship in perfect working order. "Of *course* it's working. *Rock Dragon*'s ready whenever we are."

"Oh, my," Em Teedee said. "I do hope you aren't planning any emergencies. In future, I suggest that we avoid any adventures that might involve emergencies. Far too dangerous, if you ask me."

"Come on, Em Teedee," Jacen said. "We've upgraded your capabilities. Don't you want to test your limits?"

"Indeed not," the little droid said from his place at Lowbacca's belt. The Wookiee chuffed and patted the droid good-naturedly.

Tenel Ka's face remained solemn during this exchange—then again, she usually *was* serious, Jacen thought, even though he constantly tried to make her laugh. "I am ready for whatever circumstances dictate," she said. "We are now required to look at the fire and listen to Master Skywalker."

"This is a fact," Jacen said with a chuckle, repeating Tenel Ka's own oft-used phrase.

Earlier that afternoon, a ship had come in bearing a pair of Jedi Knights who had been trainees when Luke Skywalker founded his Jedi academy here. The two Jedi visitors, exhausted from a dangerous mission they had just completed, had gone quickly into the temple to refresh themselves. Not long afterward, Luke had announced a celebration for that evening. Jacen wondered eagerly what his uncle intended to talk about.

Now the fire blazed high. Orange flames crackled through the pile of dead wood; spicy-smelling smoke wafted upward from the burning lichens and mosses that clung to the underbrush. While the last few Jedi trainees made their way to their seats, Jacen played with a small bluish-green frill lizard he had found making a nest out of a mound of dry leaves in a crevice between the Great Temple's stone blocks.

The lizard appeared content to sit on Jacen's left fist, but seemed much less comfortable with Jacen's opposite hand. Every time he brought his right forefinger close to the lizard's nose, the creature flared out an intimidating scarlet frill around its neck and flapped its scales in self-defense. When Jacen pulled his finger away, the frill went back down. He moved his finger close again; the frill reappeared, and the lizard's eyes opened wide.

Tenel Ka watched with interest. The lizard-skin armor she wore clung to her body and glittered in the firelight. Though the night would be cool, the warrior girl never seemed to require any more warmth than the supple armor provided.

As a hush fell over the crowd gathered by the ancient pyramid, Master Skywalker stepped in front of the bonfire. The flames blazed higher behind him. He stood silhouetted in warm light, just a normal-sized man, despite the fact that he had changed the fate of the entire galaxy.

"We're all here because we are—or want to be—Jedi Knights," Luke said.

"Except for me, of course," Em Teedee said primly, and Lowie shushed him with a growl.

"Jedi Knights protected the Republic . . . but it is important for us to think about whether being protected is always good." He paused to let that sink in. Tenel Ka frowned, and Jacen tried to think of a circumstance where protection might not be desired.

"We learn from our mistakes," Luke continued. "And sometimes, if we shelter people from *all* the bad things that can happen, they don't learn to protect themselves . . . and even greater tragedies may occur."

During this speech, Zekk quietly joined his friends on the ledge. One arm was bandaged. Lowie rumbled a question, but Zekk just gave a secretive smile and focused on Master Skywalker.

"I grew up on Tatooine," Luke said. "A desert planet with two suns. I was the foster son of my uncle Owen, a poor moisture farmer who had little happiness in a life filled only with hard work. Aunt Beru spent days at home watching the farm while my uncle and I checked our moisture vaporators, or went into Anchorhead or Mos Eisley to get supplies we couldn't buy from Jawa traders.

"Uncle Owen knew who I was: the son of Anakin Skywalker, whom most of you remember as Darth Vader. My uncle knew I had the potential to be a great Jedi, but he wanted to protect me. He tried to keep me from my dreams because of the risks I might encounter along the way. He was doing what he thought was best for me.

"My uncle was a sad man, with great guilt on his shoulders. He knew what Darth Vader had done, and—because he was afraid for me—he spent his life protecting me on that desert planet. His heart was in the right place . . . but if he had succeeded, think of the outcome: I would still be a moisture farmer on Tatooine, the Empire might still be in power, and there would be no Jedi Knights."

Luke looked up. His eyes glittered in the firelight, though most of his body was cast in shadow. Perched on the stone blocks beside Jacen, Tenel Ka nodded. He sat closer to her as his uncle's point became clear to him.

"Challenges and diversity make us strong. Too much protection can prevent us from learning, from reaching our potential. We can learn from others, but we must also learn from our own experiences . . . and our own mistakes," Luke said. He smiled. "Just try not to make too many of them before you learn."

Another figure emerged from the base of the temple, a young man with dark hair and squared shoulders dressed in a black jumpsuit and a cape. The sleek Jedi outfit looked comfortable, service-able, and well-worn.

"Master Skywalker is right. And some of us certainly made huge blunders before we managed to come back to the right course," the young man said.

"This is Kyp Durron," Luke announced with a broad grin, "one of my first students here at the Jedi academy, many years ago. Han Solo rescued him from the spice mines of Kessel, and he came here to learn the ways of the Force."

Kyp nodded at the audience with a grim smile. Firelight splashed across his face. "I came here to learn, but I was impatient. I listened too closely to the spirit of an old Dark Lord of the Sith, Exar Kun, and I'm sorry to say I caused quite a bit of trouble for the new Jedi Knights."

"Like me," Zekk murmured.

"So did I," another voice said as a second man emerged from the temple. A nimbus of wild white hair floated around his head and fluttered above his thin beard. He wore a vest and breeches with so many pockets that Jacen thought he probably could have carried all the components for his own starship engine inside them.

"That's Streen," Jaina whispered, and Jacen immediately recognized the man. Once a cloud prospector on Bespin, the old hermit had developed an affinity for controlling the weather and the winds.

Luke said, "These two have been Jedi Knights for well over ten years now. They learned from their mistakes and their successes, and they've served the New Republic admirably." Kyp Durron and Streen looked both powerful and exhausted, as if they had come through some terrible ordeal that had made them stronger—though neither seemed ready to tell the story.

"Looks like they've had some interesting adventures," Jaina observed.

Lowie rumbled thoughtfully. Zekk nodded.

"I, for one, do not wish to hear about them," Em Teedee said. "I've heard quite enough horrifying stories about Jedi adventures in Mistress Tionne's legends." The silvery-haired instructor was a Jedi scholar and minstrel, and had also been among Luke's first trainees.

"Then I guess Tionne'll just have to make up some songs about the new Jedi Knights," Jacen said.

Tenel Ka nodded. "Soon there will be many Jedi Knights; we must remember our heroes."

Jacen brought his finger close to the lizard again. It flashed its scarlet frill and raised up on its forelegs. The frill spread about the creature like a tiny cape. A sudden thought occurred to Jacen. He glanced over at his sister and knew she was thinking the same thing: Kyp Durron had been a very close companion of Han Solo's.

"Think Dad knows Kyp is on Yavin 4?" Jaina said.

Jacen gave his sister a sly grin. "Well, there's no reason we can't send him a message. Hey, you never know—Dad might even come for a visit."

# 2

AS IT TURNED out, Han Solo was already en route to Yavin 4 to visit his children when he got word of Kyp Durron's arrival on the jungle moon. Since he had just finished his business on Kashyyyk, he calculated the fastest possible route for the *Millennium Falcon* and, with a bit of fancy piloting, got there in record time.

With a discerning eye, Jaina watched the battered light freighter descend. She had spent plenty of time honing her own engineering skills and studying the mechanics of how starships worked. By now, the *Falcon* was one mass of repairs and replacement parts. Sections of new hull plating had replaced old blaster-scarred shields. She wondered how many— or how few—of the ship's original components remained. Many fancier ships were available to Han Solo, but the *Falcon* held such a special place in his heart that Jaina knew her father would never get rid of it.

Jaina noted that the repulsorjets seemed stronger on the starboard side than on the port side, causing the *Falcon* to sway as it landed. Fortunately her father was a superb pilot and knew full well how to compensate for any eccentricities of his beloved craft.

A flock of stubby-winged avians swept above the overgrown temple ruins toward the deep jungles. They flew in a triangular formation, emitting deep hooting sounds, like a broken Kloo horn. Jacen watched them pass. Jaina could tell that he was trying to identify the species of bird—and probably wondering if he had ever caught one for his menagerie.

When the boarding ramp extended, Jacen and Jaina rushed across the weedy clearing, and Han Solo emerged from his ship wearing a big grin. Jaina expected to see Chewbacca standing behind him, the tall, hairy form that her mother had once reportedly called a "walking carpet." Instead of the huge Wookiee, though, only her little brother came out. Anakin was slight of build, quiet, and dark-haired, a year and a half younger than the twins. Their brother did not usually attend training sessions at the Jedi academy at the same times Jacen and Jaina did.

"Anakin!" Jacen said, and their younger brother beamed.

Jacen and Jaina hugged their father. At sixteen

they both felt a bit old for such displays of affection, but Jaina got little enough time to see her father, and she enjoyed every moment of it.

"Hey, kids," Han Solo said. "I was on my way here when I got your message. Your mom couldn't break away from the Senate, but I got an interesting assignment and figured it was a good excuse for a Solo family outing."

"Aww, and I thought you came just to see me," Kyp Durron called, walking from the temple to the landing field and waving. The dark-haired Jedi Knight looked thoroughly refreshed now after a night's rest and a change of clothes.

Streen had gone off by himself to enjoy the solitude of the jungle. Jaina remembered that the old cloud prospector liked peace and quiet more than anything else.

Upon seeing his friend, with whom he'd gone through so many adventures back when the twins were just small children, Han Solo's face lit up. He came forward to clasp Kyp Durron in an enthusiastic embrace. "How you doin', kid?" He pounded Kyp on the back.

Kyp smiled. "Not so much a kid anymore, Han."

"Yeah, Dad—you've got kids of your own," Jacen pointed out.

"And *we're* hardly kids anymore either," Jaina said.

Han gave a dismissive wave of his hand. "You'll

always be kids to me. All of you. Even your uncle Luke." He seemed barely able to contain his excitement at seeing Kyp as they walked from the *Falcon* back toward the Great Temple. "What've you been up to? I haven't seen you in . . . since, ah . . ."

"It's been a long time, Han," Kyp said. "I've been off saving colonies, slaying monsters, rescuing the universe . . . you know, the usual. Master Skywalker sends most of the Jedi he's trained out on missions, while our friend Tionne stays here and helps him handle the youngsters." He jerked an elbow toward Jaina. "Like these."

Jaina flushed, and her brothers both laughed.

"Heard about your fight with the Leviathan of Corbos," Han said.

"That was a tough one," Kyp answered. "Kirana Ti, Dorsk 82, Streen, and I really had our hands full on that mission. But Jedi Knights expect to face challenges like that."

Han smiled. "I know some younger Jedi Knights who've run into quite a few challenges of their own." He tousled Jacen's hair, and the young man flinched.

"Dad, I'm not a little boy anymore."

"Uh-oh. That mean you're too old to go with me to the Blockade Runners Derby on Ord Mantell?" Han raised his eyebrows at his twin children.

"You mean *the* race?" Jaina said. She had heard of the annual spectacle, one of the grandest, most daring races a pilot could enter. It was an honor just to compete in the Derby.

Han nodded. "The *Falcon* won it three times already during my smuggling days. But this time I'll be going as a representative of the New Republic. Folks running the Derby sent in an official request, asking for me as their Grand Marshal." He gave his wry grin. "How could I refuse?"

Jaina laughed. "I doubt they could've kept you from that race if they put a few Imperial Star Destroyers in the way."

Han Solo squared his shoulders. "Hey, my wife and kids aren't the only ones who enjoy facing some challenges every now and then."

"I wish I could go with you, Han," Kyp said, stopping at the base of the looming stone temple. "But Streen and I may have to leave again in a few days. Even though Master Skywalker trains more Jedi every year, the New Republic is a big place. There are lots of missions to send Jedi Knights on and not enough of us to handle all the situations that need our attention."

Han turned to his three children with mock sternness in his expression. "Well, I'm not letting you kids go on any missions for the time being. You're coming with me in the *Falcon*, and your assignment is to have some fun. Some . . . quality time together, a family vacation. You're gonna love the Blockade Runners Derby."

Lowbacca, walking down one of the Great Temple's exterior stairways, let out a loud Wookiee bellow of greeting. Perplexed, Jaina bit her lower lip and turned back to the *Falcon*.

"I know Mom couldn't make it, Dad, but where's Chewie?"

"Ah. Chewie'd been talking about visiting his family, you know. And I'd been talking about spending some time alone with you kids. So when this Derby thing came up, I suggested now might be a good time for Chewie to take that vacation back to Kashyyyk. Dropped him off on my way here," Han answered, then lowered his voice and gave her a conspiratorial wink. "Besides, that means I need a good copilot for a while. Know anybody I might be able to use?"

Jaina perked up. "*Me?* You'd let me help fly the *Falcon* at the Derby?"

Han gave her an appraising look. "You've certainly got plenty of experience. I'm awfully proud of you, you know. If it's not too much of an imposition . . ."

"What are we waiting for?" Jaina asked.

"It's a deal then?"

"Does that mean we're entering the race?" Jacen said.

"Naw, I'm not a contestant this time," Han said. "I'm strictly at the Derby in an official capacity. My hotshot days are well behind me, since I'm, well . . .

respectable now. Anyhow, your mother sure wouldn't want me taking any chances with you kids."

"No. Of course not," Jacen said with mock seriousness.

Kyp gave Han a curious glance. "You've got that look in your eye again."

"I think he's got a plan," Anakin said quietly.

Han gestured toward himself, his face the picture of innocence. "*Me?* How can you think such a thing of your father?"

"He's got a plan," Jacen and Jaina said in unison.

Han shrugged. "Least I've got a good copilot. We'll stay here for a few hours while you kids pack. Kyp and I have a lot to catch up on. Did we ever tell you about the time he stole the Sun Crusher and went after the Imperials, as if he could take on the whole Empire with his bare hands?"

"Yes," Jacen answered quickly.

"You told us," Anakin said.

"Plenty of times," Jaina added.

"Well, it's a good story—about what *not* to do," Kyp said hurriedly, his cheeks turning red. "I've learned a lot since then."

"That's a relief," Han joked. "I'd rather not have to chase you again from one end of the galaxy to the other." He turned back toward his children and draped his arms across their shoulders as they all walked into the cool shadows of the temple's interior. With flashing lights and a bleeping sound

Artoo-Detoo trundled forward to meet them. Han reached around Anakin and patted the droid's domed head in greeting.

"It'll be good to spend some time alone with the family. Just my kids and me," Han said. "A quiet, relaxing vacation."

"Oh, I doubt that, Dad," Jaina said. "From what I hear, there's always something interesting happening on Ord Mantell."

# 3

EVEN IF JACEN wasn't entirely thrilled about leaving his close friend Tenel Ka behind for a few days, Jaina reveled in the chance to fly beside her father as his genuine copilot. Although she felt dwarfed by the huge seat that normally accommodated a burly Wookiee, she handled the *Falcon* with as much expertise as she did the *Rock Dragon*.

So far it was one of the best times she had ever shared with her father. Young Anakin, with his ability for grasping problems and solving complex puzzles, studied the navigational charts and considered various paths through hyperspace, until he announced that he had found a perfectly safe shortcut to Ord Mantell.

After Han Solo double-checked Anakin's calculations, he announced that he saw no reason not to try the new route. If his son was right, the new path would cut a full six standard hours off their transit time.

Once the *Falcon* was in hyperspace, Han said to his children, "Ord Mantell's in the middle of nowhere, but that's not necessarily a disadvantage. A lot of smuggling traffic goes through there. Its position makes the planet about equally close to anyplace else along certain hyperspace paths. So even though it's not exactly convenient, Ord Mantell makes a good way station or stopping point."

"If it's a smugglers' hangout, you probably spent some time there between Derbies—right, Dad?" Jacen asked. "Before you became respectable, I mean."

Han Solo laughed. "Plenty of times, Jacen. I never tried to hide my checkered past from you all. Doesn't seem to bother your mother anymore. After all, I learned some of my most useful skills when I was a smuggler and a crack pilot—even studied at the Imperial Academy for a while. All that stuff in my past is part of who I am; the things I learned made me a vital asset to the Rebellion when we fought the Empire. I don't spend time regretting what I've done in my life, so long as I can use it now to help the people I love."

Jaina raised her eyebrows. "So if *we* ever do anything you think is dumb, you'll understand, right? You'll just accept it as part of our growth and training?"

Han knitted his brows. "Uh, that's not exactly what I meant."

Jacen stood leaning against the back of his father's chair in the *Falcon*'s cockpit. "Tell us what you did on Ord Mantell, Dad."

"I ended up there pretty often when I was a smuggler. Seems like every time I went to Ord Mantell I ran into one bounty hunter or another, and every one of 'em meant trouble. One of the worst was an insect creature named Cypher Bos, a mercenary, as vile and self-centered as they come. He was impersonating his identical hatch-mate brother, who was a Rebel sympathizer. But all those bug-people look alike, and I couldn't tell the difference. Cypher Bos sold us out and almost captured your mom and Luke and me. Then the three of us nearly got fed to the Imperials by a cyborg bounty hunter named Skorr. They just never learn." He shook his head.

"But one of the worst pinches I ever got into was against a tough smuggler named Czethros, and his Rybet henchman Briff. They were licensed bounty hunters, as well as black-marketeers in the Ord Mantell system, and had some connection to Black Sun. When Chewie and I were in a tight situation once with the *Falcon*, we had to land on Ord Mantell and get repairs. The system was crawling with Imperials, but we made it without getting stopped.

"When Czethros found out I was on Ord Mantell, he and his pal set up a trap, kidnapped Chewie."

Han gave a halfhearted grin as he relived the memory of his bygone adventure. "Told me to give myself up for the reward, or he'd kill my Wookiee friend."

"So how did you get away?" Jacen said.

"Turned the tables on 'em, of course. I'd been keeping an eye on Czethros through some smuggler friends and found out he and Briff were taking an unmarked skimmer out to the place where I was supposed to give myself up. I stole Czethros's own ship from its hangar bay, did a few things calculated to make the Imperials mad, then led them on a merry chase on my way to the exchange point."

"Must've been quite a ride," Jaina said.

Han grimaced. "Not one I'd like to repeat. I made it to the rendezvous with just enough time to hide before the stormtroopers showed up and nabbed Czethros along with his Rybet buddy. He claimed total innocence, of course, but the ship obviously belonged to him. The stormtroopers searched the ship and found plenty of . . . irregularities. Weapons, drugs, and so on. While they were busy, I managed to sneak over and free Chewie. Next thing we heard, the Imperials had carted Czethros and Briff off to the spice mines on Kessel. I think his henchman worked some kind of deal a year later with Moruth Doole, a Rybet who worked on Kessel. From what I've seen in recent reports, Czethros is actually something of a respectable businessman on

Ord Mantell these days. 'Course I'd bet my left repulsorpack module that he's still heavily into the smuggling business."

"Aren't you afraid he might try to cause trouble for you while we're there?" Jaina asked. "He could still be holding a grudge."

Han blew air through his lips. "Not a chance. Been too many years. It's all lava under the bridge by now." But Jaina noticed a twinge of concern on his face.

She turned toward the navigation controls. "Time to drop out of hyperspace. We should be pretty close to Ord Mantell."

Han looked over and smiled at his youngest son. "Well, Anakin, let's see how your calculations worked out."

Jaina was pleased to see, as they dropped out of hyperspace, that the *Falcon* was already so close to the correct position that they were able to slip into orbit with only minor course modifications.

Ord Mantell was a bland planet of average size, with average gravity, and an average atmosphere. Its topography showed the usual landscape variations— mountains, forests, and swamps. Skeins of clouds embroidered white patterns in the sky below. However, for orbital convenience and launching maneu- vers, much of the equatorial band across the continents had been settled and converted into spaceports that boasted large docking bays and no-questions-asked cargo-handling policies.

Ord Mantell had some of the most lenient banking laws in the New Republic, famous for their flexibility. Banks there would accommodate anyone, in any line of business. As long as customers didn't cause trouble, or at least didn't get caught—and remembered to pay the appropriate landing fees, tariffs, and permit taxes—bankers never interfered.

Han looked over at his daughter. "Ever piloted a ship down from orbit all the way into a docking bay?" he asked.

Jaina brightened. "Nothing as big as the *Falcon*. I've done it with the *Rock Dragon* quite a few times, though."

"Well then, this'll be no problem for you," Han said, but his lopsided smile twitched slightly, as if he were nervous. Jaina pretended not to notice. "Go ahead and take her down."

Jaina used the copilot controls to alter their vector and plow into the atmosphere at a shallow angle. While they descended, Anakin helped her to locate a landing beacon from the docking bay at which Han had reserved a berth for the *Falcon*. He programmed in their landing coordinates.

The atmosphere shone blue on the equator as they dove closer to the surface. Jaina watched the silver-white belt of development that girdled the world resolve itself into a bustling metropolis filled with blocky prefab buildings, large flat rooftops, and countless balconies that extended out far enough for small private craft to launch secretly in the dead of night.

"Most of those buildings don't have addresses," Han Solo explained. "On this planet, if you don't know where you are and where you're going, then you don't belong there."

"How do people find their way around?" Jacen asked.

"It looks challenging," Anakin said.

"Except for the Derby, Ord Mantell's no place for tourists," Han went on. "People don't come just to hang around. You can get a lot of things done here if you happen to be willing to bend a few rules—but sightseeing isn't one of them. This planet's mainly for passing through, a place to pick up cargo or get a new assignment. Imperials used this system for fleet training maneuvers because the outer planetary orbits are so hazardous. The cometary cloud's pretty thick—that's where the course is for the Blockade Runners Derby."

While Han rambled on, Jaina sweated. She gripped the controls in preparation for landing the big Corellian ship. She didn't know why she suddenly felt so anxious, but her hands grew damp with perspiration as she brought the *Falcon* in. Maybe she just wanted her father to be proud of her. Gusty winds swirled around the tall blocky building in the center of her scope. Far below, red, blue, and green ground cars crawled along; illuminated skimmers soared between the buildings in skyward alleys.

"Just take it easy, Jaina. You're doing fine," Han said.

"Yeah, don't sweat it," Jacen said. "We trust you."

Jaina paused and let her confidence build, despite the warble of uneasiness she had heard in her twin brother's voice. She took a deep breath.

"Well, what are you waiting for?" she muttered to herself, and brought the *Falcon* down toward the big flat rooftop outside the landing bay.

As she approached, running lights illuminated a rectangular slit that yawned open, wide and dark. "Those're the docking doors, Jaina. You have to float down below. Our berth is in the upper bay."

Jaina swallowed. She had thought just landing the light freighter on the rooftop would be challenge enough; now she had to slip through this narrow hole that, from this height, looked barely a meter wider than the *Falcon*'s hull. She couldn't let anything happen to her dad's ship.

"May the Force be with you," she heard Jacen whisper. Then she remembered that her uncle Luke always told them to use their Jedi senses in addition to their training in any skill.

She was a good pilot. And she was a Jedi. She drew a deep breath, let her body relax into the seat. The *Millennium Falcon* became part of Jaina, an extension of her mind, and she could sense the distance to the outer walls. She slipped the light freighter between the opening doors without so much as a wobble or a jitter.

Han looked at her in proud amazement. "That's very smooth, Jaina."

"Just tell me where to land," she said. Her fingers danced across the repulsor engine controls. Her calm voice betrayed none of her uneasiness.

"Over there." Han gestured, and she saw a broad docking bay where a group of people stood waiting to greet them. Amber lights flashed, and someone holding bright laser torches directed the *Falcon* to its landing place.

With a final hiss, the landing pads touched down on the deck plates. Jaina felt a thrill of exhilaration. What had she been so worried about?

Han hugged her.

As they all unbuckled their crash restraints and stood up to head for the landing ramp, Han said, "Wonder who's in our welcoming committee."

"They could've hired musicians . . . maybe some kind of a band," Jacen said. "You *are* an official representative of the New Republic."

"Not only that," Han said, brushing the front of his vest. "I'm Grand Marshal of the Blockade Runners Derby. That's a pretty big honor around these parts."

Han Solo, along with Anakin, Jacen, and Jaina,

hurried to the landing ramp—only to find a group of armed soldiers blocking their exit. Looming in front of them was a tall, broad-shouldered man who wore a cape and blasters at his hip. Close-cropped moss-green hair covered the top of his head. A band of metal, inset with lights and sensors, encircled his head like a ring around some pale-green planet. The front half of the silver metal band was a visor that completely covered his eyes. The rest of the metal band appeared to be permanently affixed about his ears and the back of his skull. He seemed to be receiving a continuous flow of information through the apparatus, and his lips curled in a sneer. A constantly moving cyberoptical laser sensor burned through a thin slit in the narrow visor, glaring at all of them.

Han Solo stopped in his tracks. His confident expression quickly faded. "Czethros!" he said, a look of disbelief in his eyes.

The sinister-looking man lifted his chin, his gaze frozen in a metal glare. "Han Solo," he said in a rough, gravelly voice. "I knew if I waited long enough, you'd return to Ord Mantell."

# 4

THOUGH HAN FOUGHT to keep a calm expression on his face, Jacen sensed the sudden wave of apprehension rippling through his father. The guards looked tense, ready to fire.

Han had long since stopped carrying a blaster at his hip—a good thing, Jacen supposed; otherwise they'd probably be in the middle of a shoot-out right now. His father had been hoping for a calm family outing while he did a bit of official work for the New Republic as a special guest at the famous race. They hadn't been prepared for anything like this.

Then Czethros stepped forward and surprised them all by extending his thickly gloved hand. The skin on his face rippled as his lips twisted in a smile. "Welcome back to Ord Mantell, Solo. A lot has changed since you and I were . . . opponents those many years ago."

Eyes narrowing just a fraction, Han Solo reluctantly slid his hand into the former smuggler and bounty hunter's grip. "Uh, yes . . . that's right," he said, still cautious. Jacen felt the thick uneasiness in the air. He, Jaina, and Anakin looked at each other in confusion.

"Back then, I was an officially licensed bounty hunter. You were a posted Imperial target," Czethros said. "Nothing personal, of course. No hard feelings."

"Of course." Han flashed the metal-visored man one of his most charming lopsided grins. "I thought after all those years in the spice mines you might, uh, hold a grudge."

"It's the nature of the bounty-hunting business," Czethros said. His laser-red cyber-eye drifted left and then right. "I used every trick to apprehend you, and you used every trick to get away. You just happened to have one more trick in your repertoire than I did—at the time, at least."

He stepped back toward the gathered guards. "But I'm no longer in that line of work. I have a thriving business here on Ord Mantell. In fact, I pulled a few strings to get you selected as Grand Marshal for the Blockade Runners Derby. Since you'd settled down and weren't likely to be one of our contestants this year, I thought you might want to participate in some small way . . . if only to see what you're missing."

"Thanks, Czethros," Han said, polite but uncertain. "I appreciate the gesture."

Moving in unison, the formal guards spun about on their heels. Their machine precision reminded Jacen eerily of trained stormtroopers.

"I've assigned this honor guard to escort you to your quarters, Solo. Tomorrow is the big opening rally, and the *Millennium Falcon* will be the 'pace craft.' You'll run through the course before any of the actual contestants. The honor is always given to a pilot who has demonstrated great bravery and skill . . . in the past."

Shoulders back, head held high, Han walked close to the former bounty hunter. "Well, it's all just a bunch of show, if you ask me. Limp gundark noodles."

"But the spectators love it," Czethros said, without looking at him. "Remember your old glory days, when you were one of those hotshot pilots . . . a long time ago?"

Han stiffened, but said nothing as Czethros continued. "The course changes each year due to orbital mechanics, and we've mapped out a particularly convoluted obstacle path. I think it will make this year's Derby the most exciting ever."

"I'm familiar with the routine," Han said in a clipped voice. "I've won the race three times, remember."

•   •   •

Jaina and Han Solo spent the next morning in the docking bay facilities fully reconditioning the *Falcon*'s hyperdrive and coolant systems, as well as its maneuvering jets.

When Jaina assured her brothers that the repairs were under control, they retired to a corner of the docking bay. Jacen produced a programmable holo-projector puzzle and tried to concoct intricate designs to stump the younger boy, but Anakin managed to solve each 3-D maze before Jacen could come up with a new one.

Han stubbornly resisted most of his daughter's attempts to recalibrate the systems, but she won out eventually, after demonstrating to him that the ship really would be safer and would fly more precisely. "Chewie's going to have a fit," he mumbled, but didn't quite manage to conceal his proud smile.

Finally, when the time had come for their exhibition run through the space course, Jaina signaled for her brothers to join them in the ship. In less than a minute, Jacen and Anakin were fastening themselves in with crash restraints as Jaina sealed the boarding ramp and Han powered up the repulsor engines. From the *Falcon*'s cockpit, Han informed the Derby officials they were ready.

"Hang on, kids," Han said. He was clearly not comfortable to be the center of so much attention as Grand Marshal of the Blockade Runners Derby, but he was also just cocky enough to want to show off for all the spectators.

"It's just a little practice trip," Jacen said. "No big deal." Both Jaina and Han turned to look at him with mischievous glints in their eyes.

"We *might* have to execute a few fast turns," Jaina said.

"Just to make it more realistic," Han added.

"'Execute,'" Jacen said. "I'm not sure I like the sound of that."

Anakin gave his brother a teasing look. "Nervous?"

"Don't worry, we've got everything under control," Jaina assured her twin.

Together, she and her father worked the *Falcon*'s systems, moving like an experienced team. Jaina could sense what her father intended to do, and she realized she might indeed have the makings of a great copilot.

"Hey, where does a full-grown bantha sit?" Jacen asked.

Jaina groaned and rolled her eyes, but Anakin played along. He answered in a serious voice, as if this topic had been of a lifelong concern to him. "I've always wondered about that—where *does* a full-grown bantha sit?"

Jacen chortled. "Anywhere he wants to!"

Jaina reached behind her seat to give her twin a

good-natured swat as the comm speakers crackled to life.

"This is Ord Mantell docking control to *Millennium Falcon*," a voice announced. "We are ready for you to begin."

"We're coming," Han said as the *Falcon* drifted up through the rooftop hatches. The bright sunlight in Ord Mantell's open sky splashed across the hull, gleaming through the cockpit windowports.

As Jaina's eyes adjusted, she saw that the blocky, drab buildings were now festooned with colorful banners. Bobbing repulsorspheres floated in the air, trailing narrow metallic streamers. Rainbow-hued tassels, like levitating balls of tangled ribbon, flitted about in flocks. Jacen cried out with delight. "Hey, they're alive! I've heard of them—Ord Mantellian flutterplumes."

Jaina could see that the tiny ribbons were indeed alive, drifting like clusters of colorful worms in the air.

The voice over the cockpit speakers grew louder, as if shouting to millions of other listeners. "The Ninety-Third Annual Blockade Runners Derby is about to begin! Please welcome the *Millennium Falcon*, piloted by General Han Solo, three-time winner of the Derby!"

The cheers drifting up from the rooftops below sounded like a distant avalanche. Small one-person fliers drew close to the *Falcon*, shoving holocams to the viewports and taking pictures as the ship cruised along. Han grinned and waved at the nearest Holo-Net news reporter.

"Didn't expect such a big send-off," Jaina muttered.

Han grinned at her. "Guess we'd better give them a show worth watching." He punched the sublight engines, and a blue-white glow flared from the rear of the *Millennium Falcon,* pushing them forward. They arrowed up into the sky, leaving the holocams and the crowds behind. Their journey would be broadcast, though, by remote observer cams planted in buoys all along the route to record the race.

Jaina called up the course diagram and displayed it in three dimensions so that Anakin and Jacen could study it to find any potential points of difficulty Han and Jaina might have missed. The Blockade Runners Derby ran up out of the orbital plane into the tangled, diffuse cometary cloud that surrounded the Ord Mantell system like a distant bubble made up of mountains of ice and rock.

Frequently, gravitational perturbations from nearby star systems or planetary alignments would knock some of these tenuously held comets loose from their holding patterns, and the comets would fall down toward the sun. As they heated up, the gases would evaporate, stretching out into wispy tails of dust and ionized gas, making beautiful sights in the Ord Mantellian sky. But out here, in the deep cold of space, the comet chunks were dark, erratic navigational hazards, as dangerous as a swarm of piranha beetles.

During the Blockade Runners Derby, ships weaved through the tumbling ice cloud, ducking around and through protocomets. Speed and skill counted for everything . . . including a ship's survival, of course.

Leaving the planet's atmosphere, Han Solo increased the *Falcon*'s speed. He roared up at full acceleration, straight out of the ecliptic and into the cometary cloud. Jaina felt the skin on her cheeks pulled back by gravitational force as the engines labored. She was glad they had just tuned them up.

"Why so fast, Dad?" Jacen said from his seat in the rear. "We're just a slow, sedate pace craft, not an official contestant."

Anakin said in a level voice, "I think Dad's just trying to get some of the frustration out of his system."

"Not exactly," Han said to his sons. "We're running through the course, but"—he raised his forefinger—"they're also recording our time. So wouldn't it be wonderful if the old *Falcon* happened to do better than any of the actual contestants? How could the real winner ever live down his shame?"

"Or *her* shame," Jaina said.

"Or *its* shame," Jacen added.

"I get the point," Han said. "I intend to beat even

my last speed record, when I actually won this thing."

"Is that breaking the rules?" Anakin asked.

"Naw. But it'll give the crowds something to talk about for years." Han worked the controls, increasing speed again. "Hang on, everybody. Comet cloud ahead."

Jaina adjusted the controls, activating the newly installed windowport filters. "I'm increasing infrared pickup," she said. "There's not much reflected sunlight out here, but this way we'll be able to detect the comets a little better."

Suddenly the view changed color as they hurtled forward. Glinting, tumbling specks became visible like a cloud of sparks drifting toward them. In the holographic projection of the cometary cloud, a dotted line wove like a needle and thread through the loosely packed cluster of ice fragments.

"All right," Han said. "Get ready for some tricky maneuvers."

Almost before Jaina realized it, they exploded into the blizzard of ice chunks. Some were nearly round, some blocky and geometric, others spiny with crystalline formations.

Han gave a howl of delight as he spun the *Falcon* around. Jaina watched the engines while Anakin monitored their course. They skimmed low over one ice field, then looped around. The comets were so small and light that their weak gravity had little effect on the ship's navigation.

A tiny fragment of ice too small to be detected on their sensors evaporated against their deflector screen in a sparkle of light. More bright flashes appeared as the *Falcon* continued without slowing.

"Hey, it's like we're in a snowstorm," Jacen said.

"More like a hailstorm," Jaina said. "Those little bits of ice would poke holes right through us at our speed if the deflector shields weren't working."

"You did tune them up, didn't you?" Jacen asked.

"Naturally. Nothing to worry about."

Han focused ahead and plowed through a gaping cave in a fragile ice latticework, a comet that looked like crystal straws melted together. One of the tiny shafts struck the deflector shield and snapped. The entire cave opening began to collapse as the *Falcon* soared through and burst out the other side. But the comet's gravity was so low that it would take well over an hour for the avalanche to complete itself.

"I'm increasing speed," Han said.

"Dad, you're already close to the red lines," Jaina warned.

"And close to beating my record, too. Let's keep on with it, but keep your Jedi senses alert for anything unexpected."

"We will," Jacen said with conviction.

"We always do," Anakin added.

The ice boulders spun around as they whipped

through a denser orbit. Jaina spotted holocam buoys mounted on some of the ice chunks, and she knew that thousands of spectators on Ord Mantell were even now watching their flight. By now everyone would see that Han Solo was recklessly trying to break his speed record, and that his kids were helping him. Jaina smiled to herself. She would just have to make sure her father didn't get embarrassed.

"Let's tighten the course," she said, looking at the projection. "Gravity calculations show we could come even closer to that next comet, make a sharper turn to shave off a bit of distance here and increase our speed, whip around this hazard, come out in a backward spiral, and pull up."

"Yeah. That might make just enough difference," Han said with a grin.

They soared so close to the rotating ball of ice that Jaina could have extended the landing ramp and scraped a long gouge across the ice field.

"This is just like when we ran through the rubble field of Alderaan," Jacen said.

Ahead, four large fragments drifted close together where one comet had broken into loosely attached boulders. Han narrowed his eyes, and Jaina scanned the motion of the chunks.

Anakin watched them intently. "I see the pattern," he said. "We can go straight through—if you time it right."

"At full speed?" Han said.

"You're going to have to," Anakin answered.

Han roared ahead, straight toward the apparent blockade, but Jaina could see the comets moving, opening up. She saw the gap spreading and wondered if it would be wide enough to allow their ship to pass through.

"I've got a bad feeling about this," Jacen said. Jaina thought her brother was making a joke with their father's oft-used phrase, but as they approached the broken comet, she felt uneasiness herself.

"Yes, something's wrong," Anakin said.

Jaina watched the fragments moving, plotted their course again. It would be tight, but it seemed clear they would make it. The ship entered the slowly opening gap between rocky mountains of snow. Their deflector shield sizzled, vaporizing some of the snow and ice away from the broken comet.

"If you're worried about something, kids, tell me now."

"It's not the comet, Dad," Jaina said. "It's . . ." Then she looked up at the enhanced infrared filter and saw an array of small artificial objects, a matrix of tiny spheres, hovering just outside of the broken cometary hulk.

"Hey, what are those?" Jacen said.

"Space mines," Anakin answered in a maddeningly calm voice.

"Punch it, Dad!" Jaina cried. Han Solo reacted instantly, hammering at the emergency thrusters.

The *Falcon* was already sailing at twice the expected speed for the pace craft, and now it went into an overdrive launch.

Jaina grabbed the navigation controls herself and yanked the ship to one side, putting the *Falcon* into a tight corkscrew that plowed through the array of space mines like a drill bit. They zoomed by so fast Jaina barely caught a glimpse of the deadly explosive devices as the cluster detonated.

The *Falcon* roared away as fast as the shock wave accelerated toward them. Fourteen of the space mines blew up behind them. Jaina could count them through the rear sensor screens. When it struck, the shock wave knocked them about, but they were already tumbling. The *Falcon* narrowly missed another large comet as Jaina regained control in the copilot's seat.

"Space mines!" Han cried. "How did they get out here? This is the Derby course! It's supposed to be completely mapped and checked out before anyone ever flies it."

The *Falcon* slowed, recovering, and Jaina, Jacen, and Anakin all looked at each other. Han gasped, "If we hadn't been traveling so fast, and you kids hadn't warned me in time, we would've been right in the middle of that cluster when it exploded. But you dodged it, Jaina. Good piloting. And our speed helped us outrun most of the shock wave."

"But the course should have been clear and safe," Jacen insisted.

"That's why they have a pace craft, isn't it, Dad?" Anakin said suddenly. "To prove that the course is safe for the contestants?"

"Sure . . . but it's always been just a formality. Until now."

Jaina shivered and gripped her crash restraints tightly. "You mean maybe somebody put the explosives there on purpose—knowing the *Falcon* would be the first ship to fly through."

# 5

AFTER THE "ACCIDENT," Han Solo circled back to collect debris from the space mines and deactivate two unexploded duds. The pieces would serve as evidence of the explosions and help them to find out who had set the trap.

"I guess this ruined your chance at a record-breaking time," Jacen said as the ship headed back toward Ord Mantell. Jaina and Anakin scrutinized the exploded bits of metal and the unmarked casings, careful not to contaminate the pieces so that they could be analyzed more thoroughly later.

"Hey, we're alive," Han said. "That's more important than any speed record."

When the *Falcon* landed back on the rooftop receiving area, Czethros and several other concerned representatives rushed forward to help the Solo family disembark. The crowds of spectators who had witnessed the explosion were in an uproar, and the people sent up a cheer as Han Solo and his children gave a confident wave to show that they were all right.

A nervous-looking race official approached Han, bowing and stammering. "Oh, I'm most sorry, sir! This is terrible! We have, of course, postponed the Blockade Runners Derby at least until tomorrow. We've already sent a crew of freelance inspectors up to comb through the obstacle course in search of any other hidden traps."

"This was a near-tragedy. We must not risk anything worse happening," said a second official.

Czethros stood tall, sunlight making his green hair look like a moss-covered boulder. "I doubt the inspectors will find anything," he said grimly. "My guess is those mines were originally being taken to Anobis, a planet in the next system that has been engaged in a civil war for decades now. They frequently order weapons from black-market dealers on Ord Mantell." The Derby officials flushed in deeper embarrassment.

"Hey, how could space mines from some civil war land right in the middle of the racecourse?" Jacen asked.

"The war's still going on, and has been for almost thirty years. Many of Ord Mantell's smugglers work as gun runners to supply the war effort." Czethros shrugged. "Those mines could have been part of a dropped shipment, or even a trap set for former space authorities before Ord Mantell became more enlightened and allowed freer trade."

"Uh-huh," Han said.

The following day, after the brief and frantic postponement, racing officials attempted to relaunch the Blockade Runners Derby with renewed fanfare. Looking forward to the day's festivities with subdued eagerness, Jacen, Jaina, Anakin, and their father ascended a tall observation tower above the docking buildings.

Bald, pink-skinned Bith band members followed them, playing stirring and dramatic music to mark the beginning of the Derby. The crowd cheered. The ever-present HoloNet news reporters made repeated references to the Solo family's miraculous escape from deadly explosives the previous day.

Inside the observation tower, Jacen sat next to his sister and younger brother, while most of the reporters focused their attention on General Solo. The huge windowscreens were transparent to allow the gathered VIPs an unobstructed view across the landing centers and docking bays of the Ord Mantell strip. Once the Blockade Runners Derby began, most of the screens would turn opaque and show images transmitted from the holocam buoys. This would let everyone follow the haphazard progress of the contestants in their assorted souped-up ships as they roared through the tangle of the outer cometary cloud.

Several lavishly dressed racing officials hovered near Han Solo, preoccupying themselves with insignificant details. Han looked somewhat out of his element, uncomfortable in his formal clothes. "Since I already flew the course once, what exactly do you want me to do here as Grand Marshal?"

"Well, whenever you're ready," one of the bureaucrats said, fluttering perspiration-damp hands in the air and indicating a single red button on a panel, "we need you to push this button."

"That's it?" Han said.

"It's a very important task," the bureaucrat answered, blinking in surprise. "It's how we start the race."

Han gave him a lopsided grin. "Well then, I'll be sure to do my best."

"No need to worry, sir," the bureaucrat said. "So far, in the ninety-three-year history of the Derby, only two Grand Marshals have failed to do it correctly."

Jacen couldn't imagine how anyone could possibly manage to push a single button incorrectly, but then he'd seen some pretty disastrous bungling of simple matters in the course of his adventures.

"All right then, let's get this over with," Han said, his finger hovering near the button.

"No, no! Not yet," the bureaucrat insisted.

"You said, whenever I was ready," Han reminded him.

"But we have to send the thirty-second warning to the contestants first. And the HoloNet reporters need to get into position." The bureaucrat frantically twiddled some dials and punched codes into a small yellow touchpad.

In the observation tower several of the broad windowscreens dimmed, now displaying transmitted images of spacecraft up in orbit. Other contestants remained on landing pads as a second wave in the breakneck race through the cometary obstacle course. All ships would be clocked, and the winner would be determined by the fastest time through.

Han grinned. "Did I ever tell you kids how I made the Kessel run in under—"

"Yes," Anakin broke in.

"How could we *not* know, Dad?" Jacen said. "It's one of the most famous things you've ever done."

Han brushed his fingers down his vest. "I wouldn't say that, exactly. I mean, saving your uncle Luke countless times, infiltrating the Death Star, freeing your mom from an Imperial prison chamber, helping defeat the entire Empire, exploring unknown worlds—"

The bureaucrat interrupted him. "*Now* you may proceed, sir," he said. "All ships have been informed and are ready to begin."

Han stepped forward to the red button and extended his finger. "This button, right?"

"Yes, that's the one."

"You're sure I'm doing this properly?"

The bureaucrat did not pick up on his sarcasm at all. "You seem to be performing most admirably."

"Good," Han said. He pushed the button. The Blockade Runners Derby began.

Ships roared off pell-mell, choosing their own preferred routes to the cometary cloud, some swinging around the planet for a gravitational boost, others heading in a straight-line path, still others taking an incomprehensibly convoluted course.

The holocam buoys captured some of the contestants as they streaked by, an odd assortment of supercharged vessels, modified so that the pilots could withstand excessive acceleration; some ships had heavily reinforced shields to allow them to rip through the course without worrying about ramming into a few comets along the way.

Jaina stared at the viewscreens, her face filled with fascination. "Look at the range of spacecraft!" she said. "Skimmers, freighters, courier vessels . . . Dad, I don't even recognize some of those vehicle types."

"Anybody with a few spare parts and some ingenuity can create their own new vehicle type," Han said. "Done it myself a few times."

A new ship flashed across the screen so rapidly

that though Jacen thought for just a moment that he recognized the configuration, he decided it must be just his imagination. After all, he'd been daydreaming about Tenel Ka. It was only natural. Even though he was glad about being able to spend some time with his father, he also missed the young warrior girl.

And Lowie, too, of course . . .

Since the discovery of the space mine cluster on the course, several contestants had dropped out. Han had commented that they must have been too fainthearted in the first place and it was no great loss. Now only the toughest, most seasoned pilots remained in the race.

The ships jockeyed for position, jostling each other and nearly causing a few collisions as they tried to find the best routes that didn't intersect each other. The vehicles scraped by far closer than their collision-avoidance systems should ever have allowed, but most of these crack pilots had probably shut off their warning systems anyway.

One viewscreen showed a graphical representation of the race. Blips with code numbers traveled through the obstacle course on the grid. Jacen could watch the progress of the contestants by tracking the colored lights. Some blips moved forward; others fell behind. The holocam buoys, while an ingenious idea to cover the race, nevertheless provided only infrequent snapshots at discrete points—not enough images for anyone to follow the entire spectacle.

A Sullustan *Vector*-class spaceskimmer went slightly off course, and careened into the comet field. The buoy holocams caught the image as the skimmer struck an icy protrusion, then went into a spin. Enhanced deflector shields protected the pilot from instant death, but the ship was knocked completely awry, and the Sullustan pilot, disoriented, zoomed away in the wrong direction.

A pair of Corellian single-occupant fightercraft swept along opposite sides of a comet and nearly collided with each other at the other end. They spun out. One ship crashed in the ice field, its pilot ejecting in a lifepod at the last moment and sending out a distress beacon. To their credit, race officials reacted instantly, dispatching medical droids and rescue craft that waited just outside the cometary cloud.

"I wish Lowie were here to see this," Jaina said, still fascinated by the dazzling images of the great race.

"And Tenel Ka," Jacen said, narrowing his eyes. "She must be thinking of us. I feel like I'm sensing them somehow—as if they're closer than we think."

On the gridmap of all the racing ships, Anakin pointed to one blip that was slowly passing every competing vessel. "This one will win," he said. "I can tell by the piloting, by the speed. It has already overtaken most of the others that were launched first, and this ship entered the race near the end. It won't crash, either. I'm sure of it."

Outside in the streets of Ord Mantell, spectators watched the flat unmarked walls of square buildings that had been turned into transmission screens to carry images from the buoys scattered along the racecourse. Elsewhere in the New Republic— particularly in gambling casinos such as those in Cloud City on Bespin, cantinas on Borgo Prime, and various other legal and illegal meeting places— people placed bets on the Derby's outcome.

If Jacen had ever decided to gamble, he would certainly have taken his younger brother's recommendation. Anakin had an uncanny ability to predict things such as this. He watched the blip creep past several other racers as the ship zoomed through the cometary debris.

"Who is that contestant?" Jacen asked. He looked down at the code number, but it meant nothing to him.

The bureaucrat came over, all smiles. "That one qualified at the last minute." He rubbed his hands together in a nervous gesture. "And it looks as if we were correct to let them enter so late. The pilot seems most skillful."

The mysterious ship passed two more competitors, swooped around a large comet, then zigzagged through the toughest part of the course. The craft moved in time with the broken icy space debris, reminding Jacen of an intricate dance. The ship and the comets seemed to be cooperating, moving as one connected system. He had never before seen anyone fly with such sensitivity to the surrounding environment and obstacles.

The ship hurtled around the last comet and then looped back toward Ord Mantell and the finish line. The time displayed on one of the screens was better than any of the other competitors had clocked. No one would be able to beat it.

As the craft zoomed past the last holocam buoy, Jacen and Jaina watched the blur. Jaina recognized it almost immediately, but took a moment to put her thoughts into words. "That . . . that's a Hapan passenger cruiser. I recognize the design."

"It's Tenel Ka!" Jacen said. "And Lowie. They must have a great pilot."

"I've never seen Lowie fly that fast," Jaina said.

"Well," Han said, "they certainly won the race."

The bureaucrat stood up. "Come, Han Solo. You are the Grand Marshal. You must be on the upper platform to greet our winners as they arrive back from the cometary cloud. The other ships will straggle in, but you must be there to wave and shake their hands . . . or appendages."

"Well, somebody's got to do the job," Han agreed.

"We're going along," Jacen replied. "If that's

Lowie and Tenel Ka in the *Rock Dragon*, I want to be the first to see their faces."

The bureaucrat glanced at him after checking the race contestant records. "I'm afraid you may be mistaken. No one by the name of 'Lowie' or 'Tenel Ka' is registered as the pilot of this vessel."

"We'll just see for ourselves," Jaina said.

A turbolift took them to the top of the observation tower, and then a floating platform shuttled them across the crowded rooftops. The hastily erected grand stadium stood by itself, garlanded with beautiful feathers, flowers, and the colorful flutterplume creatures that Jacen had identified.

Jacen shaded his eyes and looked up at the azure sky until he saw a glint of the ship appearing from high orbit, cutting through the gusty winds. The pilot unerringly found the reception platform and the waiting celebration. Jacen and Jaina waved, recognizing the Hapan passenger cruiser that Jaina herself had flown so often with Lowie at her side as copilot.

"You're right, kids," Han Solo said. "That's the *Rock Dragon*. No doubt about it."

When the small ship settled down, dozens of new floaters surrounded the stage and platform, holocams and curiosity seekers. In the distance, cheering crowds of humans and aliens stood on rooftop landing pads, in ship hangars, and on balcony flight decks, waving banners and shouting. Jacen could already see other contestants coming in to land, now fighting for second or third place.

But when the *Rock Dragon*'s hatch opened and a figure emerged, Jacen was astonished to find that it was neither Tenel Ka nor Lowie.

"Zekk!" Jaina cried. Behind Zekk, her other two friends stepped out and stood next to their new dark-haired pilot.

Tenel Ka gave only the faintest smile upon seeing Jacen—then again, she never gave more than a faint smile about anything—but Lowie bellowed loudly, raising a ginger-furred fist in victory. He seemed immensely pleased that the *Rock Dragon* had won the prestigious daredevil race.

Zekk's emerald eyes flashed, and he gave his friends a warm smile. "Just following Master Skywalker's instructions," he said. "He told me to find something I was already good at, and try to use my Jedi skills to become even better. I've always enjoyed piloting, so I thought a hotshot race might just be a good test."

"And it was indeed quite a challenge for us all," Em Teedee chirped, sounding exhausted.

Jacen looked around at his friends. The crowd cheered the winners, but all that mattered to Jacen was having the young Jedi Knights back together again.

**6**

TOGETHER AGAIN, THE young Jedi Knights learned how to deal with being celebrities. Jacen, Jaina, and Anakin had already spent a lot of time with their father in his duties as Grand Marshal of the Blockade Runners Derby, but now that Zekk, Tenel Ka, and Lowie had actually won the race, publicity seekers and HoloNet reporters pestered them constantly, taking their images, interviewing them, asking them what it was like to receive such an honor.

In the history of the Derby, no crew so young had ever won the challenge. Upon discovering that these were Jedi trainees, some of the losers cried "foul," claiming that the use of the Force gave an unfair advantage—though the *Rock Dragon* had not taken advantage of the permitted mechanical modifications, as most of the other contestants had.

Fortunately the controversy died down quickly.

The newspeople had other planets in the galaxy to dash off to, and Ord Mantell preferred to keep media attention to a minimum. Large groups of organized smugglers—some of them rivals, some allies—were a powerful political force, and they managed to shoo away the reporters shortly after the Derby ended.

Some of Ord Mantell's most prestigious "businessmen" (important smugglers, Jaina presumed) had invited Han Solo to a banquet to thank him for his work as Grand Marshal, no doubt in an attempt to curry favor with the husband of the New Republic's Chief of State. Jaina smiled as she thought of this possibility: her father had nothing to gain by taking bribes, but she doubted the smugglers would realize this. Jaina wondered if Czethros would be there.

Meanwhile, the Solo children spent the afternoon with their friends in the docking bay where the *Falcon* was berthed. At Han Solo's request, Zekk had been allowed to dock the *Rock Dragon* in the same secure VIP bay where Jaina had landed the *Falcon*, so that the Grand Marshal's ship and the Derby winner were isolated and protected in the same security area.

When the twins told their friends about their adventure during the trial run of the obstacle course, Tenel Ka immediately suspected an assassination attempt. The warrior girl tossed her red-gold braids and squared her shoulders, obviously ready for action. She'd had plenty of experience with political intrigues in the tough environment of the Royal House of Hapes.

Lowie expressed concern and Em Teedee dutifully translated, though Jaina could already make out many of the ginger-furred Wookiee's words. "Master Lowbacca suggests that we look at the space mine debris. Perhaps with some attentive analysis, we can determine the mines' origin."

"Good idea, Em Teedee," Jaina said absently, then looked up into Lowie's golden eyes. "I mean, Lowie."

The little translating droid detached himself from Lowie's fiber belt and floated in the air on his microrepulsorjets, bobbing about the docking bay. They went to the storage locker near the *Falcon*, where Han had insisted on keeping the evidence, believing that only he and his New Republic technicians could be trusted to perform a thorough analysis.

"For some reason," Jaina said, "Dad isn't too confident that the people on Ord Mantell will give us an honest answer."

Jacen said, "They're probably more interested in keeping their smuggling records secret."

"Secrets are fine," Zekk said, "except when one of those secrets holds the key to who tried to kill you."

On a worktable mounted to the docking bay wall, Jaina spread out the twisted fragments that had been scooped up by the *Falcon*'s tractor beam. The young Jedi Knights pressed closer. Not much remained after the mines' detonation and vaporization in space, but Anakin scrutinized the shrapnel carefully and began to sort the pieces into piles he knew went to individual mines. Jaina let her younger brother work, knowing how well he was able to solve puzzles and visualize the way pieces fit together in three dimensions.

In short order, Anakin had several partial mines reassembled. Lowie and Jaina helped him with the wiring, finding parts of serial numbers and determining the initial configuration using the two duds as a reference. The duds were dangerous, though they had been defused. If the mines had not detonated as programmed, Jaina didn't trust them to behave properly when deactivated either.

Lowie growled as he picked up some of the pieces with his long fingers. Zekk studied the shrapnel as well. "I think these are contraband war materials," he said. "So much smuggling goes on through Ord Mantell, this could have come from a black-market weapons merchant."

Jacen suggested, "Didn't Czethros say something about a civil war on a nearby planet? Anobis? The smugglers are supplying them with munitions."

"But were those mines out there just dumped by

a gun runner who was about to be caught," Jaina asked, "or were they intentionally set up to take us out of the picture?"

Jacen sighed. "With all those HoloNet news reporters here covering the race, you'd think some of them would want to do a story about that terrible war everybody's talking about."

"That would be too dangerous," Zekk said with a snort. "They'd rather do a nice, fun story about a space race."

Jaina set down one of the broken space mines and shook her head. "We're not going to find out anything else unless we learn who some of the weapons dealers are. But for now . . . I'm hungry!" She smiled at Zekk, then turned to Tenel Ka. "Don't suppose you upgraded the food-prep units on the *Rock Dragon* yet?"

Tenel Ka nodded. "This is a fact. They are now programmed to provide the best Hapan cuisine."

"Sounds good—I'm starved." Jacen said, then looked over at the warrior girl. "In fact, let me push the buttons so I can say I made you a fine lunch."

"That would be most appreciated, friend Jacen."

Ducking inside the *Rock Dragon*, Jacen tinkered with the food-prep units until they produced some kind of meal whose name he couldn't pronounce. Tenel Ka called it "authentic" and "delicious"; Jaina found it "interesting."

They laughed and talked, sharing food and friendship. Jaina especially enjoyed having Zekk as a close friend again, rather than an enemy or a guilt-ridden young man. Zekk was rapidly becoming the person she had known for so many years. No, not the same person—better. More mature.

Around a mouthful of food, Jacen said, "Hey, stop me if you've heard this one. A bounty hunter, a Jedi Knight, and a Jawa trader walk into a cantina—"

A resounding chorus of "We've heard that one!" rang through the cabin.

In the middle of a swirling gelatinous dessert that insisted on crawling around the plates by itself, Tenel Ka sat up straight and alert, her eyebrows raised as if something was wrong. Lowie also growled.

"What's up?" Jacen asked.

"I sense something," Tenel Ka said. "I would like to investigate."

She stepped out of the *Rock Dragon*, moving with feline grace, reaching out with her senses. Jaina watched the warrior girl, admiring the smoothness of her actions. Although she had lost her left arm in a lightsaber battle with Jacen, Tenel Ka had not allowed the handicap to slow her down.

The docking bay was silent, except for the hum of machinery, the ventilation system, and the distant sky traffic overhead through the rooftop doors. The bay walls were smooth gray metal. The *Millennium Falcon* sat unattended in shadows.

Tenel Ka froze for a moment, then stepped away from the *Rock Dragon,* flicking her granite-gray gaze from side to side as she walked deeper into the docking bay. Jaina stood beside Lowie at the hatch. The young Wookiee's fur bristled, and she could feel his uneasiness.

Tenel Ka stood stock still in the middle of the large room, her shoulders rigid, her arm partially bent at her side. She scanned the wall and studied the shadows, the old lubricant stains and smoke smears from hundreds of landings and takeoffs. She took three steps closer to the small workbench where the recovered space mine fragments had been spread out.

Tenel Ka waited, narrowed her eyes, listened, and finally pulled out her rancor-tooth lightsaber. Jaina couldn't figure out what the warrior girl was doing. The walls remained gray and featureless. Tension hung thick in the air. Finally, when the warrior girl held up and switched on the glowing turquoise blade . . . the shadows on the wall began to move!

Jaina gasped. Lowie surged past her and ran to help. Figures on the walls shifted, and Jaina could make out gray-skinned creatures, vaguely human-oid. They moved like spiders with angular arms and legs that allowed them to crawl up the metal walls. The colors on their smooth, clammy skin shifted, patterns of stains on the walls reflected in their body pigmentation. When they held still, the chameleon-

like creatures were almost invisible—but now that
Tenel Ka had startled them, they were more easily
seen. These shadows might be identical in color to
the walls, but the play of light exposed them.

Em Teedee cried, "Oh, dear! What *are* those
creatures? I'm certain they're not at all friendly."

One of the gray-skinned things scuttled down,
snatched up an intact dud space mine, and scrambled
back up the wall toward an air vent near the ceiling.
Another chameleon-thing grabbed two more fragments.

"They're stealing the evidence!" Zekk said.

Then all the young Jedi Knights charged toward
the docking bay wall to join the fray. Lightsabers
ignited: Lowie's molten-bronze blade that was
nearly as wide as Jaina's arm, her own electric-
violet sword, and Jacen's emerald green. Zekk, who
had forsaken his lightsaber upon returning to the
Jedi academy, now drew a handy old blaster.

Thinking fast, Anakin raced to the *Rock Dragon*'s
communications console and sounded an alarm,
calling for the authorities.

One of the chameleon-skinned creatures dropped
from above to land on Tenel Ka's shoulder, driving
her to the ground, its hands around her neck. Jacen
tackled the thing and knocked it off his friend. Tenel
Ka recovered quickly. Soon she and Jacen stood
side by side with their lightsabers, driving the
creature back.

Several other creatures ran back to the wall, pressed themselves against it, and vanished in front of Jaina's eyes. But she *knew* they were there. Zekk reached up with his blaster, turned the setting to "stun," and fired at the blank spot on the wall. Circular blue arcs rippled out to illuminate the lumpy form of a chameleon creature. It dropped like an insect sprayed with poison and curled up on the floor.

Jaina could hear the movement of soft gripping hands and feet as more of the creatures moved along. She had no idea how many of them there were, only that the young Jedi Knights were greatly outnumbered.

But they were *Jedi,* so the odds were fairly even.

One of the unseen creatures struck Jaina from behind. She whirled about, still holding her lightsaber. With a sizzle, the violet blade connected with something solid, and one of the creatures let out a hollow wail. She saw it clearly in the flash of her energy blade, its lips smooth, its mouth toothless. Patterns on its skin shifted like a thunderstorm of colors in its pain.

Zekk fired his blaster again, and a second chameleon creature fell, this time from the ceiling, a great enough height that Jaina could hear the sharp sound of hollow bones cracking from the impact.

Lowie fought in a mass of muscular, ginger-furred arms. Em Teedee cried out, "To your left,

Master Lowbacca. I sense a distortion! To your left!" Lowie turned as one of the chameleon creatures leapt. With his free hand the Wookiee smacked its soft smooth skin and belted the thing aside.

Suddenly, at the peak of the battle, Jaina saw a stranger charge into the docking bay—a young woman in her mid-twenties. She was wiry and moved like a whip. Her hair was dark, but streaked with lines like honey, as if she had woven strands of pale blond hair through her thick mane; a patterned leather band was wrapped around her forehead, holding her hair in place. Her face was narrow, her almond-shaped eyes large and dark and sad.

But what most astonished Jaina was that the young woman carried a blazing lightsaber!

The newcomer uttered a howl of challenge and ran into the fight, slashing from one side to the other, wielding her acid-yellow blade like a club. All the young Jedi Knights paused in shock, as did the chameleon creatures.

The stranger took advantage of the hesitation and attacked. She seemed able to see the camouflaged creatures, or perhaps in the young woman's wild frenzy, she struck at everything in sight and happened to get lucky several times.

Two of the creatures rippled into visibility, clutching their smoking wounds. They fell with the now-familiar hollow cries of pain before they died.

"Don't just stand there—keep fighting!" the

woman snarled, and the young Jedi Knights resumed the battle.

But with the appearance of the newcomer, the creatures' fighting resolve broke. They began to flee, a flicker of barely seen shadows.

"Hey, they're getting the space mines!" Jacen cried. Jaina raced toward the workbench as the surviving creatures grabbed the last components and swarmed up toward the air vent near the ceiling.

Jaina watched the dark shaft swallow the shadowy creatures. The young woman ran ahead with a burst of speed and leapt up at the wall, sweeping with her lightsaber and striking the last chameleon creature in the back. It fell with another wordless wail as the rest of its companions escaped.

Jaina frowned at this last needless slaughter. "You didn't have to do that. It was running, not attacking us."

"They all need to be dead," the young woman said bitterly.

Zekk and Lowie knelt over one of the fallen bodies, looking at the fading colors in the skin tone. Jaina knelt beside the one she had struck, gasping its last breaths.

"Who are you? Who sent you?" she said, but breath only rattled in the creature's inhuman face, and it died. Then she saw emblazoned in its fading multicolored skin a mark, a solid dark circle with designs around it.

She recognized the symbol. Zekk stood next to her, looked at the tattoo and then at Jaina. "That symbol reminds me of Black Sun."

Jaina swallowed hard. She knew of the legendary underworld criminal organization run by vile gangsters and evil crime lords such as Prince Xizor in the days of the Rebellion. Many other cruel leaders had also had far-reaching claws that extended into numerous activities, controlling a large portion of the most insidious crimes in the galaxy.

"But Black Sun's been quiet for years," she said.

Zekk frowned. "I wonder if they're starting up again. Or if this is something else."

Jacen turned to their unlikely helper. The wiry young woman stood there, large eyes wide, pupils dilated, body still trembling. Her arms jittered as if she were a barely contained mass of energy searching for another target to fight. Her comfortable, form-fitting shirt left her arms bare, displaying a tattoo on her right shoulder that looked to Jacen something like a piranha beetle with a lightning bolt on its back, but definitely not Black Sun.

"These creatures don't know anything. They're only henchmen, sent here to remove your evidence. Those space mines were a setup to destroy the *Millennium Falcon*."

"Yeah, we guessed that too," Jaina said. "But what I can't figure is who *you* are. Are you a Jedi Knight?"

The woman snorted. "Just because I can use a lightsaber doesn't mean I'm a Jedi. I don't need all that elite training mumbo jumbo. I can fight just fine on my own."

"We could see that," Jacen said, enthralled.

Tenel Ka narrowed her eyes. "Fighting with finesse is a greater challenge than indulging a simple battle frenzy."

The woman scowled. "Yeah? I seem to remember taking out more targets in this little skirmish than you did."

At that moment, Han Solo came rushing in, accompanied by several members of the Ord Mantell security forces. He looked around, taking in the carnage and the sight of the young Jedi Knights standing with their lightsabers still blazing. "We came as soon as we got Anakin's alarm! Are you kids okay?"

Jaina switched off her weapon. "We handled it, Dad," she said.

"I can see that." Then he noticed the young stranger, who was now staring at him, her dark eyes ablaze with fury. She stepped forward in a tense, threatening posture, her yellow lightsaber held out in front of her. "Han Solo!" she said, her voice dripping with anger.

Han looked at her, but his face showed no recognition.

"Han Solo," she repeated. *"You killed my father!"*

# 7

UPON HEARING THE stranger's shocking and sinister announcement, Jacen instinctively moved with his sister to stand beside their father. Anakin came out of the *Rock Dragon*, lifting his chin high.

"I don't know what you're talking about, young lady," Han said. "I don't even know who you are."

"You'd better explain yourself," Jacen said. "Sure, we're glad you helped us out, but how dare you go accusing my father of murder?"

The young woman did not tear her gaze away from Han Solo. Her dark, sad eyes narrowed, as hard and glassy as chips of obsidian. Tenel Ka, Lowie, and Zekk also stood beside Han, but the young woman did not seem to care a whit about being outnumbered. She still held her flickering lightsaber as if ready to take them all on.

"My name is Anja," she said, her voice cold and even. "Anja *Gallandro*."

Jacen watched his father flinch and draw back. His expression fell, and he swallowed hard. Jacen blinked, surprised at the guilty reaction his father had shown. Was there something to what this young woman had said?

"You . . . you're Gallandro's daughter?"

"In the flesh," Anja said. "I was just an infant when you murdered my father."

"Wait a minute." Han held up a hand. "I didn't kill Gallandro."

"I'm surprised you even remember him," Anja said bitterly. "With a career like yours, the way you stepped on your competition, cheated people, dumped your spice loads at the first sign of Imperial patrols, no wonder you've had a price on your head for most of your life."

"Of course I remember Gallandro," Han spluttered. He looked around nervously at the Ord Mantell security troops who had come with him to investigate the alarm, at the dead chameleon creatures that lay strewn on the floor. Han didn't seem to notice that the space mines had been stolen.

He said to the troops, "Clean up this mess and . . . report everything to the authorities. I want to file an official complaint." He tossed his dark hair back. "My kids were threatened. They could have been hurt."

"How touching," Anja said.

Han marched briskly toward the *Millennium Fal-*

*con* with a strong gesture. "Come with me. We'll talk inside the *Falcon*, where we can have a bit of privacy." He strode up the boarding ramp and did not look back.

Jacen turned to his sister, and they shared a hard glance. Then all the young Jedi Knights quickly followed Han into his beloved, battered ship. Anja sniffed, drew a deep breath, and switched off her lightsaber. She clipped it at her side. After waiting for them all to board the *Falcon* ahead of her, she followed them up, wary, as if suspecting a trap.

Han slumped heavily into a seat in the small recreation lounge, with its scratched and dented hologame table in the center. Equipment, spare parts, and leftovers from various cargo trips hung in the supply bins and nets. The ship looked lived in, comfortable and messy, like a familiar bedroom that wasn't cleaned up any more than it had to be. Jacen knew that their mother Leia never made any demands on Han Solo's upkeep of the *Falcon*. This was his private area, and he could do what he wanted here, so long as it was safe.

"You can't lie to me, Solo," Anja said, preferring to stand despite the empty seats available. Instead, she watched him, then paced around the room looking at Han's mementos and trophies of missions he had flown.

"I've spent my life learning about my father. My mother told me some stories before she died, and there are plenty of records in the Corporate Sector Authority archives."

"Well, your father was a hard one to forget," Han Solo admitted. "He was reputed to be the fastest draw in the galaxy. Challenged the clan leader to a duel on the planet Ammuud, but when I was picked as his opponent, Gallandro declined to fight me."

Anja snorted in disbelief. "There was more to it than that. My father was working for the Corporate Sector Authority to break a slaving ring. Slavers you were involved with, Solo."

"I didn't know!" Han said. "Anyway, I'm the one that got all the records the Corporate Sector needed to convict the ringleaders."

"But then you overwhelmed my father, humiliated him, and fled justice so you couldn't be charged for the crimes you had committed."

Han looked at his children, who stared back with questions in their eyes. "Hey, that was a long time ago—and I didn't really do anything wrong."

Anja laughed bitterly. "Nothing wrong? How about when you killed my father?"

"But," Han insisted, "I didn't kill him. I wasn't even there. He had stunned me, and then went off—"

"Hah. You were in the buried derelict *Queen of Ranroon*, searching for the lost treasure of Xim the Despot. My father and you had agreed to work together to find the hoard that had been hidden thousands of years before the rise of the Old Republic. But when you finally discovered the treasure vaults, you double-crossed him. Shot him in the back, from what I hear."

"No. That's not true," Han Solo said, his face drawn and angry now.

Jacen looked back and forth, from the stern, troubled anger of the young woman to his father's baffled yet clearly guilt-ridden denial.

"It wasn't my fault," Han said.

"And a few years later, I was left an orphan on war-torn Anobis. My father had come through Ord Mantell many times. He met my mother on nearby Anobis just as the civil war was starting. They fell in love, but he wasn't home much because he had his missions to accomplish. My father did great work as an agent for the Corporate Sector.

"But from one mission he never returned home. My mother was devastated. My planet was being ripped apart by a civil war caused by the Imperials and the Rebellion—and she died in despair, a widow. *You* took my father away."

"Hey, I didn't kill your father. Gallandro was responsible for his own death. He made a choice, and let down his guard. . . ." Han struggled to find the right words. "He set himself up for what happened."

"Yeah. And you shot him," Anja replied.

Han Solo spread his hands but seemed to see the

futility of making any further protestations. Jacen wondered why his father couldn't just convince her, why he didn't haul out proof of what had actually happened, why he didn't even explain himself fully. What did he have to hide?

Anja sniffed the recirculated air inside the *Falcon*'s enclosed spaces. Jacen suddenly noticed the sour smell of lubricants, old upholstery, numerous meals from Corellian food packs, and the metallic tang from air that had gone too many times through the oxygen scrubbers.

"You've done well for yourself, Solo," Anja said, her eyes huge and tired. "Married to the New Republic's Chief of State, three kids training to be Jedi, Grand Marshal of the Blockade Runners Derby. I'll bet you're pretty proud. But at what price did you gain all this? Everyone you stepped on along the way can see full well how you got where you are."

Anja abruptly turned and marched toward the boarding ramp. "This isn't what I expected. I had hoped for a fight. I wanted you to argue. But you, Han Solo . . . you're nothing. Compared to my father, what he was and what he did, you're too insignificant for me to kill."

"Wait!" Han Solo said with no conviction in his voice whatsoever. "There's a lot I can tell you about your father. He and I weren't always enemies, you know. More like rivals, just competitors."

"I don't want to hear it, Solo. Especially not from you." She strode out. The young Jedi Knights followed her to the boarding ramp, and Han Solo joined them as Anja stalked away from the ship.

Outside, the Ord Mantell guards and cleanup crew had nearly finished restoring the docking bay to a reasonably tidy appearance. They paid no attention to the angry young woman who hurried away from the battered spaceship.

Suddenly Anja stopped, as if gathering her nerve, and turned around to flash another angry glance at Han. "*If* you're such a champion of goodness and righteousness, Solo," Anja said, her voice laced with venom, "and if you and the New Republic really have the best interests of the galaxy in mind, why is it that for about twenty-five years—throughout the Rebellion and now during the growth of the New Republic—you have simply ignored my war-torn world? Why has Anobis been completely passed over by all of your peacekeeping and reparation efforts? Why have we received no help?" Her voice was choked with emotion.

Jaina turned to her father. "I never even heard of Anobis before we came to Ord Mantell," she said.

Anja continued, hurling the words at him like weapons. "Anobis began to fight with itself in the last days of the Empire when the agricultural plains villages took up the cause of the Rebellion, hoping to overthrow Imperial rule. The mountain mining villages, though, required interstellar trade to survive and wanted to maintain the stability of the Empire. Thus a civil war began, with Rebel sympathizers and Imperial sympathizers tearing each other apart. It's never stopped, and our world is now one big scar."

"But the Rebellion's been over for decades," Jacen said. "How could it still be an issue? The Emperor's long dead."

"And my people are still fighting. Only now they're fighting for a cause rather than for reality. You should go to Anobis, Solo. Take a good look at what's happening there. *If* you can tear yourself away from such important diplomatic duties as watching space races or waving banners in the winner's circle."

She glanced one more time over her shoulder. "Why don't you find out where your help is really needed? If you're brave enough to accept the challenge."

The Anja marched away, leaving Han Solo and the young Jedi Knights behind, flustered and disturbed.

## 8

PUTTING THE DESPISED Han Solo behind her, Anja hurried away from the docking bay, moving faster than she had expected. Emotions surged through her, and adrenaline flooded her body. She had been warned that the encounter might affect her strongly, but she now found herself relishing the moment she had anticipated all her life.

The setup had been perfect, and Solo's reaction was priceless. Guilt had been written like a brilliant holographic billboard across his face. Even his own children would have to doubt him now.

Oh, how she hated the man. Anja gripped the lightsaber hilt that hung at her waist. Her fingers spasmed. She stretched out her hand in front of her and watched her fingers tremble until she forced a calm upon them. *Calm . . . calm.*

She stepped into a turbolift that took her down to the lower levels of the tall, nondescript warehouses.

She paced inside the enclosed lift, feeling like a trapped animal. With a clenched fist she pounded on the metal wall, but the slow repulsor engines took no notice of her frustration. She gritted her teeth and breathed deeply, but the cold air held a tart and metallic smell. Sweat trickled down her temples and leaked out from under the leather headband.

Han Solo's face kept flashing in front of her mind's eye, taunting her with the thought of all the unfair advantages he had in his life—his three delightful children, his beautiful quarters at the old Imperial Palace . . .

After an eternity, the lift doors opened, and Anja dashed out onto the midlevel connecting walkways. She glanced at her wrist chronometer. It was late. She would miss her meeting unless she ran. A feral grin spread across her face. She could handle it. She had plenty of excess energy to burn off, so she sprinted. Her small feet made light clanging sounds on the metal walkways as she turned, descended a hollow-sounding staircase, and ran between a pair of large buildings in search of the right entrance.

Because of the privacy and secrecy requirements on Ord Mantell, most buildings were not numbered or identified in any way. That proved a detriment only to people who didn't know where they were going.

And Anja Gallandro knew where she was going. Inside the echoing, complicated enclosures, she saw a host of shady-looking creatures. Some were bounty hunters or scavengers, criminals of various sorts huddling in the alleyways. Suspicious eyes gleamed at her, some on swiveling stalks, some with faceted insect eyes that captured multiple images of her figure as she flitted down one narrow alley into another. When she finally reached a sealed door with a hidden keypad, Anja punched in the code, then paced and fidgeted for the two seconds it took for the door to acknowledge her presence and slide open.

She ducked inside, hot, anxious, burning with inner energy. The door sealed behind her with a thunk. Inside, the room was dark. Anja waited, refusing to be intimidated. Her heart still pounded, and her head seemed to crackle with static from the fading aftereffects of the dose she had taken.

Suddenly all the chamber lights blazed on. Anja stood blinking, unmoving. She knew this couldn't be a trap, because her employer had had ample opportunity to kill her before—and now she had information he needed.

"So what have you learned, little velker?" Czethros said from his comfortable seat. His single cybernetic eye blazed red behind his visor.

*Velker.* At first, Anja had hated the nickname Czethros gave her after taking her under his wing and training her to be his tool, his weapon. But then Anja had learned that velkers were fearsome, fast-flying predatory creatures from Bespin. They were sleek, deadly attackers. She could think of worse things to be called.

"I learned quite a bit. I met Han Solo," she said. "I told you those old space mines you set as a trap wouldn't fool him for an instant. Now he's on his guard. I hate the man, but I respect his abilities. His children have excellent skills as well—I watched them fight." She tossed her streaked hair back, adjusted her headband, and raised her chin. "Not as good as me, of course, even though they're using Jedi skills. They don't have quite the . . . enthusiasm."

Czethros laughed. "Enthusiasm? You go into a berserker rage when you've had too much."

"It's useful sometimes," Anja said. "And I managed to drive back most of those clumsy chameleon attackers. Your work, I presume?"

"Did they get away with the evidence?"

"Easily. I hope you didn't mind losing a few of them. We had to kill about seven."

Czethros shrugged. "They're cheap. I can always buy more."

"Now it'll be harder to kill Solo," Anja said. "The one thing I'm after. You might have screwed up my chances."

Czethros laughed, though his pale, sickly-looking face showed no humor at all. He ran one hand over his moss green hair. "Solo is cocky. His easy escape from the space mines, and your resounding defeat of the chameleon creatures, will probably only make him *more* willing to jump into peril, not less. He doesn't know how to be careful. And his children seem to have even greater potential for getting into trouble than he does."

"Well, I've planted the suggestion in his mind," Anja said, getting down to business. "I taunted Solo with the desperate situation on Anobis. If he rises to the bait and blunders happily into the war there, he's doomed."

"Excellent," Czethros said. "That way my overall plan can proceed without his interference. He's one of the few people in the galaxy who can expose the enterprises we're trying to build through Black Sun."

"And, if you help me get rid of him, there can be no greater payback for me than to avenge my mother and father."

"Be patient, Anja. The time will come," Czethros said. "You've waited this long. Let's do it right."

She bit her lip and nodded. She tapped her fingers on the metal surface of the nearest table, stood up and fidgeted, looked around. "I . . . may need to go with Solo, in order to nudge a few things along." She hesitated.

Czethros watched her with his cybernetic red laser eye, waiting. The cruel streak was coming out in him. He had to know what she wanted, but he twisted the screws, making her *ask* for it. For what she needed.

She drew herself up again, trying not to look weak. "But in order to be at my peak performance, as this mission requires, I'll need . . ." She trailed off. He *knew* what she meant.

Czethros continued watching her. "Yes?"

Anja felt a flash of anger, and pounded her fist on the metal wall with a dull clang. "I need my supply! I used my last dose of spice in order to fight your clumsy henchmen."

Czethros laughed and then made a *tsking* sound. "You seem so desperate. Don't worry, little velker. You can count on me." From his pocket he withdrew a sealed black case and held it aloft, just far enough away that she would have to step forward and reach out to take it from him.

He tried to toy with her, pulling it back, but Anja moved too quickly. Still in the aftereffects of her hypersensitivity, she snatched the case before he could play his little trick. Czethros covered his surprise at the speed of her reactions.

"There's your supply of andris spice," he said. "You're taking too much of it, you know. I can't keep up this rate of payment without further results."

"You'll get results," Anja said, checking the contents of the tiny carbon-freeze box. Each of the small cylindrical containers inside was wrapped in an insulated covering. Exposing the andris fibers to deep cold intensified the effect of the spice. But she didn't *need* another dose now—though she wanted one very, very badly. She would keep the samples, hoard them, take them only when she needed the spice.

When she needed it more than she did now.

Without a word of thanks or goodbye, Anja turned and slipped back out of Czethros's hidden warehouse. She would keep a close watch on Han Solo, and insinuate herself into his journey to Anobis. She was almost certain he wouldn't be able to resist going there now that she had challenged him.

And once he got there, he would be very surprised indeed.

# 9

BACK IN THE diplomatic suite of Ord Mantell's most luxurious hotel, the Ord Ambassador, Jacen could not get his mind off the girl Anja. Her sad, pain-filled eyes had seemed so out of place. Her features were delicate and beautiful . . . and there had been such a strength in her whip-thin body that Jacen had expected her gaze to be as steady and cool as Tenel Ka's. But her personal pain—perhaps even a slight madness—had been all too apparent in the looks she had given Jacen and his friends.

Zekk had felt it too, because Jacen had seen the older boy's sympathetic nod when Anja spoke of her father's death, and about having been raised as an orphan. Who would understand better than Zekk how such events could change a life?

But Jacen didn't have Zekk to talk to right now. The former Dark Jedi had returned with Tenel Ka and Lowie to the *Rock Dragon* for the night.

Jacen sighed and ran his hands through his tousled curls. Why couldn't he stop thinking about Anja? He paced restlessly about the central chamber of the suite. After the long day today, Jacen had taken a hot sonic shower, but his mind did not feel refreshed. Something was bothering him, and he couldn't quite put his finger on it. When his brother Anakin entered the room, hair still damp from his own shower, the younger boy's ice-blue gaze stopped Jacen in his tracks.

"Something's wrong," Anakin said. A statement, not a question. Startled, as always, that his younger brother could sense things so quickly, Jacen hunched his shoulders and plopped himself down on a stone repulsor bench beside the ornamental firepit in the center of the room.

Anakin perched himself on a bench opposite Jacen and stared into the flames. "She was a very interesting person, wasn't she?" he said quietly, then waited for Jacen to answer.

Jacen glanced sharply at his little brother and stared at him for a full minute before the reason for his inner turmoil clicked into focus. "Dad never really explained what happened to her father," he finally blurted. "He just evaded her questions with vague answers."

"Well, he said he didn't *kill* Gallandro. What more do you want to know?" Jaina asked, gliding into the room and helping herself to a seat between her two brothers. She wore a loose robe, and droplets of moisture still sparkled on her cheeks from her recent bath.

Jacen set his chin stubbornly. "I want to know what happened."

Anakin shrugged. "Then let's ask Dad."

"Ask me what?" Han said, entering the room, a white sheet of absorbent material draped around his neck so that it hung down his bare torso. He took a seat opposite Jaina and between his two sons; the four Solo family members were like points of a compass, with the artificial fire at their center. Jacen glanced at his sister. She bit her lower lip. Anakin gestured to him, as if to say, *This is your question; ask it.*

Jacen knew he might sound rude, but he wanted an answer and he didn't know how else to put it. "Anja said you killed her father. You denied it, but you never explained what happened to Gallandro."

Han nodded slowly. "That young lady took me by surprise. She reminded me of an incident from my past . . . a time I'm not too proud of."

Jacen wondered if guilt was the source of the hesitation he heard in his father's voice.

"So, what happened?" Jaina prompted, her brandy-brown eyes alight now with interest.

"We were looking for an ancient treasure, a lost legacy of Xim the Despot," Han began. He paused, then sat up straighter. He spread his hands as if backing up to provide more explanation. "Gallandro was a smuggler, you see. A quick draw, a sharp-shooter and, uh"—a corner of Han's mouth quirked in a lopsided smile—"a fellow scoundrel. We found where Xim hid his treasure, but Gallandro betrayed the rest of our team. Decided he wanted it all for himself. Challenged me to a blaster fight."

Jacen was instantly alert. His father had always been one of the best shots in the New Republic. "And?"

His father lifted one shoulder for a second, then gazed down into the flames. "And I lost."

All three young Jedi stared at him in disbelief.

"But you're not dead," Jacen pointed out.

"How *did* Gallandro die, then?" Anakin asked.

"His aim was good, but not fatal. He drew first, hit me in the shoulder. My shot went wide, and I dropped my blaster as I fell. While I was down he put binders on me and went off to chase one of the other members of our team, a Ruurian."

"They look kind of like miniature Hutts, don't they?" Anakin asked. "Only furry, and with legs?"

Han nodded again. "I wasn't even there when Gallandro caught up with the Ruurian. But the treasure vaults had been booby-trapped—rigged so that if you drew a weapon in certain areas, the automated defenses would take you out. There were warning lights in those areas, but the Ruurian had removed them. Gallandro never realized he was walking into a trap."

Han grimaced. "I don't know. Maybe I'd've done the same thing. The Ruurian explained it to me afterward: he figured Gallandro had nothing to worry about—so long as his intentions were peaceful. But if the guy drew his blaster . . . well, then he'd get what he deserved. Could be that Gallandro only meant to injure the Ruurian, like he did me. In any case, the vault's defenses did the rest."

Jaina squeezed her eyes shut. "How awful."

Jacen remained skeptical. "If that's the way it happened, then why didn't you just tell Anja?"

His father's eyes clashed with his. "Tell her what? That her father was a traitor? A man who turned on his own team once the treasure was found and took it from them? A hotshot blaster jockey who got fried because he thought with his weapons instead of his brain?"

Han drew a deep breath, let it out with a slow shake of his head. "Besides, I had no idea before today that Gallandro *had* a daughter—or that she's blamed me for his death all these years. With the resentment she's built up in her life, if I told her what really happened, she might just take it into her head to go after the Ruurian, Skynx, because *he* disabled the glow signals that would've warned her father not to draw his blaster."

Han's eyes filled with doubt, and he looked back

into the artificial firepit. "Still, I do feel a kind of responsibility toward her. I wish there was something I could do."

Jacen wondered if there was some additional reason why his father should feel responsible. Had he told them everything?

"Maybe there is something we can do," Anakin said.

Han sat back, a thoughtful look on his face. "Her planet, you mean?"

Jacen brightened at this idea. "That's right. Anobis isn't too far from here. And that civil war sounds terrible."

"It wouldn't hurt to go check it out," Han admitted. "In my official capacity, of course—see if there's anything the New Republic could do to help."

"Kind of a diplomatic mission, you mean?" Jaina said. "I'm sure Mom would agree to that."

A slow lopsided grin spread across Han Solo's face. "Yeah. I think she would," he said, getting to his feet.

He reached out to ruffle both of his sons' hair, then walked around the circle, leaned down, and kissed Jaina on the cheek. "You kids get some sleep now. I'm gonna get dressed, go down to a comm center, and put in an official call to the Chief of State of the New Republic."

Jacen nodded with satisfaction. It was the least his father could do.

# 10

AFTER A STRANGELY restless night populated by images of unbearably sad eyes and flowing dark hair streaked with blond, Jacen woke to find his sister standing beside the cushioned pallet on which he slept. She tossed a clean jumpsuit at him.

"Time to get up, sleepyhead. We want to get an early start."

Jacen, groggy from his lack of rest, blinked up at her. "What for?"

Just then Anakin appeared in the doorway, a travel satchel slung over one shoulder. "I'm all packed," he announced.

"For the fact-finding mission to Anobis," Jaina explained. "Mom said it was a good idea. She sent Dad a transmission this morning of everything the New Republic knows about the planet and their civil war. Unfortunately, it's not much."

The impact of his sister's words finally sank in,

and Jacen came fully awake. Untangling himself from the cushions and blankets, he leapt to his feet. "Where's Dad now?"

"Went down to the docking bay to start preflight checks on the *Falcon*," Jaina said.

"We leave in less than an hour, Jacen—if you're ready," Anakin said, running a skeptical eye over his older brother. "Zekk, Lowie, and Tenel Ka are already there waiting."

As he scrambled to get dressed, Jacen felt miraculously energetic. They were going to *do* something to help Anja's planet, he thought. Maybe they could find a way to banish the sadness from her eyes forever. The young Jedi Knights were going on a true rescue mission, just like the ones Tionne used to tell them about from Jedi legends.

He flashed his siblings a cheerful grin. "Don't worry. I'll be ready."

By the time Jacen reached the docking bay, Anakin was already at work at the navigation controls and Jaina was examining the external sublight engines. Tenel Ka, Zekk, and Lowie were gathered around Han Solo, being briefed on the upcoming mission.

Seeing Jacen, Han gestured for him to join the other young Jedi Knights. "So, if this planet is as torn up from the war as Anja says it is," he concluded, "we might just need a few extra helping hands. I think we should all stick together on the

*Falcon*, though. Got plenty of room and there's less chance of running into trouble if we don't slip up."

Jaina looked up from her work on the sublight engines. "But what about the *Rock Dragon*?" she protested.

Han glanced at the Hapan passenger cruiser. "I think we can station an extra guard or two here without much difficulty."

Tenel Ka's lips curled in a hard smile. "And the vessel has its own . . . security systems."

"Indeed, yes," Em Teedee said. "And they are most efficient. I had a fine conversation with them just this morning."

"It's settled then." Han clapped his hands and began giving out assignments.

Jacen was glad to know that all of his friends would be coming along. They worked well as a team, and he had no doubt that together they could handle anything that happened on Anobis.

He had no sooner begun his task of examining the *Falcon*'s lower hull than a familiar figure sauntered into the docking bay. She held herself straight and proud, and her dark, streaked hair trailed behind her like the tail of a comet.

"Hey, what are you doing here, Anja?" Jacen asked, managing to sound brash, if not outright rude. He felt himself turn red with embarrassment as he realized his blunder.

The young woman seemed not to notice. She bent

to look at him beneath the *Falcon*'s hull, her big eyes serious. "After what happened yesterday, I wanted to make sure that your ship had come to no harm."

"Hey, that's kind of a coincidence," Jacen said. He started to stand to get a better look at her, but only succeeded in smacking his head on the belly of the *Falcon*. He quickly ducked down again. "What I mean is, we're all on our way to Anobis—to help your people, like you suggested."

Anja cocked her head slightly as she digested this information, then shrugged as if this were no more than she had expected. "I'm on my way back there myself."

"Hey, Jacen. Don't forget to check those two rear struts when you're finished," his father's voice called from inside.

"Uh, Dad?" Jacen called back. "Do we have room for another passenger?"

"Depends. Who—?" Han jumped off the ramp to land beside the ship, and his question ended in a wordless whistle of surprise.

"Anja needs to go to Anobis, too," Jacen hastily explained, seeing the strained look that passed between his father and Gallandro's daughter. Anja backed away from the *Falcon*, drew herself to her full height, and folded her slender arms across her chest. Her attention remained on Han Solo while Jacen continued.

"I thought maybe we could give her a ride. She can probably show us the safest places to land, maybe even introduce us to a few important people."

His father returned the girl's challenging stare. "Would you be willing to do that?"

Anja gave a curt nod. "Maybe not to help *you*—but to help my people, yes."

Han gave her a hard look, as if he didn't quite trust her motives. "All right. You're welcome on the *Falcon*, then. You can tell us more about your planet's war once we're under way."

Jacen listened with fascination as Anja recounted the tale of the strife that had been raging among her people for decades, since the days of the Empire.

"And so," Anja continued, "the people of the valley who worked all of the rich farmlands declared war on the mountain people simply because we traded with the Empire. They stopped trading with us or selling us food. What else could we do?" She looked earnestly around to her circle of listeners.

"In the mountains we had no way to make a living except with our mining. If we hadn't agreed to trade with the Empire, the Imperials would have come and taken the raw materials from us by force. We had very few herd beasts, and no croplands. We would have starved."

Seeing the skepticism on the faces of his father

and his sister, Jacen could not help but come to Anja's defense. "The valley people should have been helping you. After all, it wasn't a crime just to trade with the Empire. A lot of current members of the New Republic did that."

Anja gave a sad sigh and nodded. "Not only did the farmers declare war on us, they also sabotaged our mines by booby-trapping the tunnels. They continue to do so even today. The tunnels collapse, our people are killed, and our work becomes ever more difficult."

"Yeah, well, there are two sides to every story, kid," Han said. "Maybe more than two."

Jacen thought about the story his father had told Anja about Gallandro's death, and what he had told Jacen, Jaina, and Anakin the night before. He wondered if there might not be more than two sides to *that* story as well. . . .

"We're on a fact-finding mission here," Han went on. "And we'd like to get the story from as many points of view as we can before we decide how the New Republic can help."

Anja gave him a haughty look. "Of course, I just have to *hope* you know the truth when you hear it."

Jacen wondered.

# 11

AS THEY CRUISED away from Ord Mantell, Anja sat stiffly against a bulkhead wall facing the *Falcon*'s cockpit, where Han Solo and Jaina sat at the ship's controls. Anja's face was hard, her arms folded over her chest.

Across from her, Jacen smiled. "Why don't you relax," he said. "We'll find a way to help your planet."

Anja closed her big, sad eyes and gave a mirthless laugh. "Right. A few pampered kids and one former smuggler will fix everything. I feel better already."

Lowie gave a soft growl, turning in the passenger seat to look at Anja.

Tenel Ka sat stiffly beside Jacen, as if ready to protect him. "This is not a fact. We are not children," she said. "We are Jedi Knights. We have all faced hardship."

"And war," Jaina added. "And the death of friends and family."

Zekk spoke up from beside Lowie. "And General Solo here has some real influence with the New Republic fleet."

Anja looked skeptical. "It's just hard to believe, since nobody in the New Republic has ever bothered to think of us before, much less offer us help."

"Give us a chance," Jacen said. "We're your friends—at least we'd like to be."

"With the past history between our fathers, I'm not certain becoming friends is possible," she said in a flat voice. No anger, no hope . . . no emotion at all now. Jacen watched her, wondering deep in his heart exactly what *had* happened between Han Solo and Gallandro so many years before the twins were born. "Besides," Anja continued, "the flight to Anobis is brief enough that there's little point in getting comfortable."

"The hyperspace route to the Anobis system *is* short," Anakin said. "We'll arrive in less than a day."

"Then that's when the fun starts," Anja murmured.

She removed her lightsaber and began playing with it, looking at the intricate knobs and buttons. Every lightsaber was different, made from various raw materials. Jacen, Jaina, Tenel Ka, and Lowie had built personal energy blades using their skills and their imaginations. Anja was not a Jedi trainee, yet she had a sophisticated-looking lightsaber, apparently an ancient one.

Jacen tried again to strike up a conversation. "Hey, that's an interesting weapon. Have you had any Jedi training?"

Anja threw her head back and looked at him with scorn. "I don't have time to sit around in the jungle and concentrate at rocks and leaves." She made a rude noise. "No. I bought this lightsaber from an old trader. He said it's some sort of Jedi relic. Who cares? It works. That's all that matters to me."

"But you used it well against the chameleon attackers," Tenel Ka observed.

Han Solo turned in his pilot's seat. "You don't need to be a Jedi to use a lightsaber, kids," he said, still trying to make a gesture of peace toward Anja. "Fact is, I used your uncle Luke's lightsaber on Hoth, to cut open a tauntaun so we'd have a place to keep warm until I could set up a snow shelter."

Anja looked at her weapon again, studied the ancient carvings and scrollwork on its handle. She shrugged. "I can fight with reckless enthusiasm and enough skill to overpower any opponent I've encountered so far. It doesn't matter whether the Force is with me or not."

Fifteen hours later, the *Falcon* dropped out of hyperspace at the edge of the Anobis system.

In the cockpit Jaina sat with Zekk looking over

her shoulder at the copilot controls. The dark-haired young man seemed intrigued by the systems of the modified light freighter.

"I can fly this ship," he said.

"No you can't," Han answered.

"In theory, I meant," Zekk said. "The *Lightning Rod*'s very similar, only a little smaller and designed to be flown by only one person." He looked down at the sensor array that scanned space in front of them. He pointed to the small blip just as Jaina herself noticed it.

"There's another ship sharing our course," Zekk said.

"We're approaching pretty fast. That ship doesn't seem to be in much of a hurry," Jaina said. "Must be a cargo hauler."

Zekk nodded. "It has smaller engines, a bulky design. Not built for speed. It's a cargo hauler all right."

"Better let them know we're here." Han Solo leaned forward to the comm unit and opened a hailing frequency. "Ship ahead, this is the *Millennium Falcon*. Looks like we're on the same heading. Please identify yourself."

Instead, the small hauler released a cluster of metallic spheres that drifted in space for a few seconds before exploding in a blossom of multicolored fire. Then the ship jinked to the right, altered course, and swept downward using its low-power engines. The *Falcon* dodged the debris and rapidly closed the distance.

"Space mines," Zekk said.

"Again? Does he think he's running his own Derby out there?" Jaina asked.

"We'll catch up to him in no time," Zekk said. "He's got no chance of outrunning the *Falcon*."

The pilot ahead seemed to realize the same thing. He returned to his course and responded over the comm system. "H-hello, *Millennium Falcon*. This is Lilmit, captain of the *Rude Awakening*—an officially licensed cargo hauler from Ord Mantell. M-m-my apologies for that accidental release a minute ago. Our defensive systems malfunctioned and identified you as an enemy. I trust no one was injured?"

Han grunted. He nudged the *Falcon* closer to the other ship. "What's your destination, Lilmit?"

"Anobis. I've g-got some important . . . supplies to deliver."

Anja glanced up from where she sat behind an invisible psychological wall that cut her off from the companions. She came forward to the cockpit.

"He must mean food and medicinal supplies," Jaina said, not realizing that Han still had the comm circuit open.

"N-not, uh, exactly, *Millennium Falcon*," Lilmit said. "But my c-cargo is important to the war effort, nevertheless."

Anja moved farther into the cockpit. "He's running weapons," she said. Her voice dripped with scorn.

"Lilmit, this is Han Solo, a special emissary from the New Republic. I'll be coming aboard for a brief inspection." He brought the *Falcon* so close to the small cargo hauler that their hulls nearly touched.

"Y-y-you what?" Lilmit stammered. The *Rude Awakening* put on a burst of speed that the *Falcon* easily matched. "Y-you have no right to detain my ship. I'm—I'm officially licensed."

"Then we should have no problem. Besides, I'm well aware of how much a license from Ord Mantell is worth," Han said, "and exactly how much one costs." He glanced at Anja. Her face bore a troubled expression. "Are you ready to be boarded?" he said into the comm system.

The two ships flew along side by side, nearly touching, but Lilmit still refused to answer. Han extended his grappling hook and attached the docking field. "Let's do this peacefully, Lilmit. Don't make me blast you and take over the wreck of your ship. It'd be a heck of a lot of trouble for both of us."

The other pilot mumbled something unintelligible, which Em Teedee offered to relay, but the young Jedi Knights quickly assured him that some things were better left untranslated.

"C-c-come on aboard, then," Lilmit grumbled.

"B-but you're delaying my delivery. I'm perfectly legal."

"His actions suggest otherwise," Tenel Ka said.

The docking clamp engaged with a loud metallic clank, and after a hiss of air equalization, both ships were ready. "I'm going across first, kids," Han said, taking the lead. "Just in case there's a trap."

"If it's a trap, Dad," Jaina said, following close behind him, "you'll need us next to you, not hiding inside the *Falcon*."

Han looked over his shoulder and cocked an eyebrow at her. "You know, you may be right."

He opened the hatch and quickly descended into the smaller ship. Anja's face contained a thunderstorm of anger in anticipation of what she knew they would find aboard the smuggler's ship.

Lilmit, a small grayish-skinned man, had winglike eyebrows and a wrinkled, ridged scalp. He met them with frowns and flailing hands. Jaina noticed that his fingertips were connected by thin translucent webs of skin. Finally, he forced a ridiculously fake smile onto his face.

"Han Solo! W-welcome aboard my ship," he said. "It's not in very g-good condition, but it's paid for. I've had it for many years—and this war on Anobis has been providing some of our best business since the Empire fell." He rambled on, his tone obsequious. "We've g-g-got a lot in common, don't we?

You used to be a smuggler yourself. Y-you ran spice for Jabba the Hutt, didn't you?"

"Nearly cost me my life a few times," Han answered. "It's been decades since I ran those kinds of risks for a quick profit."

Lilmit sighed. "If only we c-could kick back in a cantina on Ord Mantell, sh-share a Rhuvian fizz or some Osskorn ale. Then we'd have time to socialize."

"I'm not here to socialize, Lilmit," Han said coldly. "We're here to check out your ship's cargo."

Anja snatched out her lightsaber, switching it on so that its acid-yellow glare flooded the small compartment. "Show us your cargo *now*!"

Lilmit recoiled, holding up his webbed hands. "It's j-just my usual run! I've been doing this for years. N-n-nobody's ever bothered me before."

"Then today's your lucky day," Zekk said, standing close to Anja. The young woman, tall and slender, had a sort of animal energy that dominated the room. Zekk had no lightsaber himself. Jaina, Jacen, Tenel Ka, and Lowie did not draw their weapons, though the smuggler could surely see them at their sides.

"All right, all right. C-come with me."

Inside the cargo hold they found crates filled with munitions: blasters, burrowing detonators, sonic punchers, and other explosive devices.

"Just as I thought," Anja said. She pointed to the

box of sonic punchers. "He's taking these weapons to the enemy."

"War material is forbidden, even for smugglers," Han Solo said. "I can't remember the exact statute or regulation in the New Republic charter, but I'm sure that's the case."

"I would be pleased to look it up for you, Master Solo," Em Teedee volunteered. Lowie rumbled that it didn't matter at the moment.

Lilmit looked completely flustered. "I'm m-merely trying to make a living. There's a good m-market for these things on Anobis. There's quite a demand. P-people *need* to defend themselves."

"And which side have you chosen?" Tenel Ka said. "Which army do you support?"

"Oh, I couldn't take s-sides in a civil war," Lilmit said. "That would be unfair. I supply everybody. L-l-let them work it out. That's my creed."

Anja flared with anger, barely able to keep herself from cleaving the smuggler in two with her lightsaber. "You supply the enemy *and* our side? You sell to both equally?"

"Wait a minute," Jaina said. "Which one is 'our' side? We're just going there to investigate."

Anja didn't hear her. She turned to Han Solo. "If you really pride yourself in being a high-and-mighty representative of the New Republic, you *cannot* let him deliver these weapons. Think of how many people these munitions will kill . . . how much more blood will be on your hands."

Han drew himself up. "Anja's right. We're going to have to confiscate your cargo, Lilmit."

"You c-can't do that!" the smuggler wailed. "I've got m-mouths to feed—an entire litter of offspring back at Ord Mantell. You'd put them out into the streets! I'll f-file a complaint!"

"I happen to know it doesn't cost much more to get a license permanently canceled than it costs to buy one in the first place." Han's gaze didn't waver. "And in your case, I'd consider the credits well spent. You might want to try a more reputable line of business."

Han gestured to Lowie, who helped him lift a large crate of burrowing detonators and set it in the center of the cargo floor, just above an irising space hatch. "Let's pile these other crates on top," Han said.

Zekk, Tenel Ka, and the twins used the Force to help, while Anakin did his best to be of assistance in directing their efforts. Anja remained where she was, her lightsaber still drawn as if daring Lilmit to argue with them.

"I'll report you to the authorities on Ord Mantell," the smuggler whined. "Y-you say you're confiscating my cargo, but you'll probably fence it yourself, s-s-sell it on the black market."

"Hey, not a chance," Jacen said.

Han Solo opened up a crate and removed one of the powerful detonators. After setting its timer, he placed it back in the box and sealed it. They locked all of the cargo crates together magnetically and coded the locks to a single control. After Anakin scrambled the coded combination for him, Han stood back. "I think we'd better leave our friend Lilmit alone so he can jettison his crates."

"B-b-but there's a fortune tied up in those weapons!" the little man said. He waved his webbed hands as his eyebrows flew upward like flames to his wrinkled scalp.

Han drew his blaster and pointed toward the crate with the timer ticking down. "If I were you, I'd get rid of the cargo, Lilmit. If you don't your ship'll become the newest, brightest little star in this part of the galaxy. I can't make that choice for you, but I'm not going to wait around to see what you do." He gestured, and the young Jedi Knights hurried after him to the *Millennium Falcon*'s docking port.

Lilmit wailed, "B-but I'll never get that open in time! How m-much time did you set the countdown for?"

"Oh, a minute . . . maybe two. Can't remember exactly."

The smuggler ran to the crate, pounded on its side. "I can't g-get it open!"

"I suggest you jettison your cargo without delay,"

Tenel Ka said. Lowbacca added his growl of affirmation.

The companions scrambled back into the *Falcon*. Han headed straight for the pilot's seat and strapped himself in while Jaina released the magnetic docking connection. They split away from the smaller cargo hauler and drifted off to a safe distance.

"How long does he have, Dad?" Jaina asked.

"Plenty of time," Han said. "I think."

Finally they saw a cluster of glittering objects pop out from the bottom of the smuggler's ship. Lilmit's sublight engines kicked in, and he streaked away only moments before the jettisoned cargo containers erupted into a white-hot ball of light.

"Looks like he made the right decision," Jacen said.

"This is a fact," Tenel Ka agreed.

"Not bad, Solo," Anja said. "Your method was crude, but it's good to know you occasionally do make the right decision."

Aboard his small ship, Lilmit swung between despair and outrage. He had just lost a huge profit. It would have paid for his long-awaited vacation on Tatooine. For years he had scrimped and saved so that he could fly out under the double suns, soak up warmth from the glittering sands, enjoy the wild nightlife in Mos Eisley. Now those dreams and plans were trashed.

With trembling fingers he opened a special private comm signal. It was time to express his anger to the people in charge. Perhaps they could do something about this marauder, this space pirate named Han Solo. Lilmit clenched a fist, trying to control his anger.

The image of Czethros appeared on the screen. The angry-faced leader appeared greatly annoyed that Lilmit had bothered him. His red laser eye burned bright behind his metal visor.

"You m-must do something about Han Solo!" the smuggler blurted, leaning so close that his flat nose nearly touched the viewplate. "He and a group of kids just boarded my ship en route to Anobis. They confiscated my cargo and forced me to destroy all the weapons."

"Really?" Czethros said. "You didn't mention my name, did you? I don't want Anja to know that Black Sun is involved in her own little war."

"Of course I kept m-m-my mouth shut," Lilmit said. "But what am I supposed to do n-now?"

"Obviously, you'll have to make up for these losses."

"D-don't you think I know that?" Lilmit said. "But I want you to make Solo p-p-pay for this—in blood. I work hard, I pay my protection money, and I do whatever you ask. Now it's time for Black Sun to do something for me. K-keep the spacelanes to Anobis safe for us gun runners."

Czethros laughed, but the laser-red eye in his visor did not waver. "You can't order me around, Lilmit. You're no one, a mere underling who drives a craft and delivers boxes."

Lilmit trembled, knowing he had overstepped his bounds in talking to Czethros that way. One didn't make an enemy of the powerful crime organization without paying a steep price. Thanks to the efforts of Czethros, Black Sun's tentacles now reached into every known business in this part of the galaxy.

Then Czethros did smile; it appeared to be a genuine smile, or perhaps the man was a much better actor than Lilmit thought. "It just so happens, though, that your wishes exactly parallel mine with regard to Solo. Sort of a personal grudge of mine. Don't worry about it for now."

"But how will I g-get restitution?" Lilmit stuttered. "Someone has to p-pay for my lost cargo."

"You're absolutely right," Czethros said. "*You* do. You allowed yourself to be boarded. You didn't deal with the situation properly, and you lost the weapons. It comes out of your account."

Lilmit swallowed hard. He knew of no way he could escape his obligation now.

Czethros laughed. "If it's any consolation, Solo is walking right into the civil war on Anobis. He seems to think he can make everything better, but I've got about a thousand different ways to make sure he never leaves that planet alive."

"Well," Lilmit mumbled. "That's one thing to look forward to at least." Slumping deep into his pilot chair, he switched off the communications channel, then called up his credit records and banking tables in an attempt to figure out how he could possibly pay for the lost merchandise.

# 12

FROM THE CORNER of her eye, sitting in the *Falcon*'s copilot's seat, Jaina observed the change in Anja's demeanor after the run-in with the weapons smuggler. It seemed the thin, angry girl had gained a small measure of respect for Han Solo, though it was clear she still carried an enormous chip on her shoulder.

Then, as Han brought the ship down through the atmosphere of Anobis toward the war-scarred inhabited areas, something happened to fire up Anja's temper all over again.

She pointed to a wrinkled ridge of mountains in a temperate zone. "My mining village is down there. The leader of the town, Elis, holds great power in the loose federation of mountain villages. We should talk to him. He'll confirm everything I've said."

"But aren't they the Imperial sympathizers?" Zekk said.

Anja bristled. "That's what the *original* debate was about, over twenty years ago. Now the war has become . . . something more."

But instead of heading for the mountains, Han arced the *Falcon* away toward the flat fertile ground embroidered with rivers and green forests, square patches that had once been fields, and small clusters of homes. The farmland, now brown and abandoned, was dotted with small craters.

"I want to try talking to the people of a farm village first," Han said. "We've already heard Anja's side of the story. Let's get a little perspective."

Anja fumed. She jutted her chin forward. "You don't believe me? You think I lied to you?"

"I didn't say that at all," Han said.

"He just wants to get a different point of view now," Jacen said. "Don't worry. We'll talk to both sides."

Anja lowered her voice. "Right. More than twenty years of war and a former spice smuggler is supposed to trot in, talk to a few people, and put an end to the fighting."

Tenel Ka's voice became gruff, matching Lowie's deep growl. "Perhaps it is time someone did something to prevent your people from continuing their fighting."

"You're asking for trouble," Anja said bitterly. "Those farmers down there can't be trusted. They'll probably try to blast you out of the skies as you come in for a landing."

"Good thing we just upgraded the *Falcon*'s shields, then," Han said.

Jaina grimaced. "If we can't even land safely, how did you expect us to survive in the midst of a whole civil war?"

Anja narrowed her eyes as if this exact question had occurred to her already. Somewhat unsettled, Jaina turned back to the copilot controls and scanned the ravaged landscape that rolled past beneath them.

Anobis had been an agricultural and mining colony world, never heavily populated and somewhat off the beaten path, despite its easy access to Ord Mantell. It seemed that the colonists managed to survive well enough to build their homes and live their lives, but no one ever became rich here. *Except maybe the gun runners*, Jaina thought, since the war had continued for so many years.

Even before the days of the Empire, the miners and the farmers had traditionally been separate groups with different needs and distinctly different outlooks. From the sketchy background files her mother had sent, Jaina knew that the miners and farmers had once cooperated with each other, exchanging metals and raw materials for produce.

But the two groups had been divided by their political leanings during the Rebellion. The miners, more dependent on offworld trade, worked to maintain the status quo of the Empire. The farmers had wanted freedom instead—the ability to succeed or fail on their own merits without the angry yellow eyes of the Emperor watching them. As galactic struggles had raged and resolved themselves independently around Anobis, the colonists had battered each other, continuing to fight long after the New Republic had won its victory.

As Jaina looked out the *Falcon*'s cockpit windows, she saw a world with the potential for beauty, but with so many scars that a long time of peace would be needed for complete healing. A large forest fire burned in the hills, far from the nearest farming village. It might even have been a natural fire.

"Jacen," Han said, "try the comm system; see if you can talk to anybody down there. Let them know we're here to help, not to fight."

Anja rolled her eyes and sat back, crossing her arms over her chest. Jacen sent out repeated calls on the comm system, but received no answer.

"Doesn't mean they don't hear us," Jaina pointed out. "They might just have a receiver and no transmitter."

"Or they might be setting a trap," Anja said.

Han brought the ship in low over the largest farming village he could find. Jaina maneuvered the *Falcon* to a smooth landing not far from the cluster of rickety homes. The boarding ramp extended, and the group climbed out, blinking in the hazy sunlight of the war-torn world. In the distance, the smoke from the distant fire curled up from the hills.

The timid villagers slowly crept out of their huts, heads lowered and shoulders hunched. They gaped in astonishment and fear at the strange spaceship. Jaina and her companions lifted their hands in a wave of greeting.

Han Solo said, "I'm an official representative from the New Republic, come to investigate your civil war and to offer any assistance we can." The people remained quiet and did not venture any farther out of their shelters.

"You'd think they'd have some kind of welcoming committee," Zekk muttered. He stepped close to Jaina.

"Maybe they can't afford one," Han mused aloud.

The buildings needed a great deal of work. Every one of them had obviously been patched and rebuilt numerous times in the wake of repeated battles. Some of the walls were new; others were composed entirely of salvage and scrap. A rickety grain-storage tower barely managed to stand upright at the rear of the village.

The hazy sky was bright, the air humid and warm, smelling of smoke. Cleared flatlands extended into the distance toward a thick forest that separated them from the rugged mountains. From what little Jaina knew about farming, she suspected this should have been the peak of the growing season—but she saw only a few skittish figures out working in the fields, hopping and dodging about in a strange way that made no sense to her. No crops grew in the barren fields, only a few patches of greenery that had sprouted all on their own.

Jacen bowed and flashed a friendly smile, trying to charm the villagers. "Take us to your leader?"

Finally, several of the farmers came out. Their eyes were sunken, their faces gaunt. Some looked angry; many wore bandages from injuries.

Anja hung back, scowling, and muttered to Jacen, "I can't believe we were ever afraid of these people. They look too skittish to fight a nerf colt."

"They've probably been through a lot," Jacen said.

"So have my people in the mountains," Anja retorted.

The other villagers faced one of the central dwellings and waited until a door swung open and a broad-shouldered man hobbled out. He had obviously once been a muscular person, perhaps a great farmer who could lift his own weight in punja grain or fight herd beasts bare-handed. But now the man's skin had a pale appearance, as if he spent all his time indoors.

As he stepped forward, the man's left foot clanked on the ground. Jaina saw that his real leg had been amputated just below the knee; he wore a makeshift

replacement limb, cobbled together from second-
hand droid parts that didn't quite fit together.
Although the servomotors no longer functioned, the
man used his droid limb as a peg leg to help him
walk about as he needed.

"We don't get many visitors here," the man said,
"except for people wanting to sell us weapons . . .
or to prey on us."

"We're not trying to do either," Han Solo said.
"We want to help."

"Then I don't know what you think you can do
for us." The man sighed and clomped forward,
extending a callused hand. Han Solo took it grate-
fully. Jaina also shook the man's hand while the
others greeted him in their own ways. Anja remained at a distance, her face a mask of distrust.

"My name is Ynos," the man said. "I'm what
passes for a leader in this group of villagers, though
we're mostly starving and we don't amount to much
of anything."

"If you're starving then why aren't you out
working the fields?" Jaina asked. "There seems to
be plenty of cropland, and it's a beautiful day."

"Because we're afraid to," Ynos said, his lips
twisting in an angry snarl. "The mountain miners
have ruined all of our fertile land. There was a time
when we harvested enough to keep us fat, with
plenty left over for trading with the miners, as well

as for export offworld. Now we barely scrape by with our tiny gardens here."

He gestured to small patches of plants outside the ramshackle homes. "A few of our people have tried to clear some of our old acreage, but it's a dangerous task. The cursed miners plant burrowing detonators everywhere."

Jaina shuddered. She had heard about mobile robotic explosives that tunneled into the ground and waited there for someone—anyone—to unwittingly step on them.

"Some of our braver young men and women venture into the forests to hunt for food, but even the trees and shrubs are booby-trapped with deadly pits and trip wires. Sometimes our hunters don't come back." Several villagers sighed or smothered soft moans of despair.

"It is only a matter of time before we're all wiped out," Ynos said. "Then the mountain villagers will have won the war."

"Unless we kill *them* first," said one brash young helper.

"And then we will all be dead anyway," Ynos replied in a heavy voice.

Tenel Ka looked at the man and studied his stump of a leg. She seemed to feel a camaraderie with Ynos, though her injury had been caused by an accident, and his by an act of war. "There is no honor in such destruction. Only cowards kill those they cannot see. And only a fool kills when there are other options."

Ynos sighed and looked around at the squalid village. Jaina followed his gaze. Her heart went out to the desperate workers in the nearby fields. She saw a few figures moving slowly, taking each step with meticulous care.

A sudden wash of dread flooded through her. All the young Jedi Knights whirled and focused on the same field, sensing the danger—just as one of the distant farmers stepped forward. An explosion ripped under his feet, sending up a cloud of dust and dirt shards, along with an incinerating heat.

The scattered workers in the fields screamed. Some froze in utter terror, while others ran blindly back along the narrow, well-packed trails that led safely through the cropland. The villagers lurched into motion, rushing toward the field.

Anakin popped back into the *Falcon* and emerged a moment later carrying the medikit. Tenel Ka ran like a hunting cat, with Anja pacing her step for step, as if it were some kind of a competition rather than a race to rescue an injured man who had stepped on a burrowing detonator.

"Be careful!" Ynos shouted, limping behind them as the other young Jedi ran. At the edge of the fields, many of the farmers stopped to embrace those who had successfully made it onto safe ground. The young Jedi Knights followed the narrow footpaths.

Jaina could see where other detonators had left craters and pockmarks in the fields, uprooting precious crops, leaving their poisonous residue as a chemical stain on the once-fertile dirt.

Ahead, Jaina saw the mangled body of the man who had been hurled high by the explosion and dropped back down among the rocks and clods of dirt. His clothes were torn, his face and limbs scorched from the blast. Blood seeped from massive injuries in his legs and chest. The man groaned. Jaina and her companions rushed to his side.

"Saw it . . . ," the man groaned, "saw it coming toward me . . . jumped." He gasped for breath, and Jaina thought she could hear his ribs cracking as he inhaled. "Not fast enough. This place . . . infested with burrowers."

Han came up, panting. "Looks bad. Can we get him back to the *Falcon*'s medical bay?"

Anakin opened the medikit, but the mangled man shuddered. Blood still oozed from his wounds. A moment later, he collapsed backward with a convulsion. Jaina could tell without checking that he had died.

Just then Ynos hobbled up on his mechanical leg and looked down at the dead man. He assessed the injuries with narrowed eyes and nodded grimly. "Perhaps it's best he died quickly. He'd never have recovered, and he would have hated being crippled."

"That is not for us to judge," Tenel Ka said. "We

cannot know what he might have contributed—
even with a handicap—had he survived."

Ynos shook his shaggy head in despair. "There
will be more deaths and injuries like this. Many
more, and there's nothing we can do about it. The
miners buy burrowing detonators and turn them
loose in our fields faster than we can clear them.
We'll never have happy lives again. We'll all
starve."

Han Solo forced an optimistic expression and put
a hand on the old man's shoulder as three farmers
gently carried their friend's body away. "You won't
starve tonight. The *Falcon* has plenty of food packs
in its prep unit. I can make you all a decent meal,
something to give you strength. It's not much, but
it's the best we can do right now."

Ynos looked at them, hunger in his eyes. Jaina
could see he desperately wanted to accept the offer.

"No argument," Han said, before the limping man
could think of anything to say.

One by one, the other villagers approached, eyes
still wide with horror at the death they had witnessed, but ready to see how Han and the young Jedi
Knights intended to help them.

# 13

BEFORE HAN SOLO and the young Jedi Knights prepared evening meal in the *Millennium Falcon*, the villagers all worked together to dig a grave for the man who had died that afternoon. They buried him in an area already dotted with mounds, and Jacen realized with shock that each mound was a grave. He doubted that many of the dead had fallen prey to natural causes.

Anobis appeared worn out and stretched to its limits, as if it were making a last gasp for life. As far as Jacen could tell, agricultural settlements such as this one continued fighting only out of sheer habit, not because of any lingering convictions. The current of hatred ran too deep to be diverted by any rational arguments.

The farmers ate the *Falcon*'s food supplies with great gusto as Jacen and Jaina served meal after meal from the galley. Tenel Ka, Lowie, and Em

Teedee welcomed guests and cleaned up after each one, while Zekk and Anakin tinkered with the food-prep unit to see if it could produce the meals faster.

The sun of Anobis set in a coppery orange glow behind the ominous mountains where the enemy mining villages were located. The smoke in the air made the colors more vivid. Keeping to herself, Anja gazed toward the craggy shadows with something akin to longing, while the farming villagers looked at the mountains with fear and loathing.

Outside, Han ate with old Ynos. The village leader seemed content that his people had received this small reprieve. "So who speaks for all the farmers?" Han asked. "Is there a council I could talk to? What would it take to bring about a cease-fire between the miners and farmers—stop all this death and destruction, even temporarily?"

Jacen paused in his serving to listen to the old farmer.

"Each of the farm communities is separate and independent, though ours is one of the largest," Ynos said, wiping his mouth. "I can speak for these people as well as anyone else. I know how they feel."

He heaved a great sigh. "You saw what happened this afternoon. It is a common occurrence. Day after day, our people are slaughtered indiscriminately by brutal weapons that strike unarmed targets. None of us are soldiers. The graveyard beyond the village is filled with the innocent victims of the miners' hatred."

Jacen saw his father shoot a glance over at Anja, his face troubled. Jacen was confused because the young woman had told a completely different story about how much pain the farmers caused the people in the mountains. He would have to assume that neither story was exactly correct.

As twilight turned into deeper dusk, the most physically fit young men and women finished eating their fill of the donated rations, then went out as sentries to guard the village. The mine-laced fields sprawled toward the forests and mountains in the west, while behind them rocky hills etched with canyons looked just as inhospitable. Night insects, birds, and more sinister-sounding creatures burbled and set up their songs around the darkening plain, particularly from the rugged hills to the east where the brushfire still glowed.

"What are you afraid of?" Jacen asked one of the villagers. "What are you guarding against?"

The gaunt young man looked at him in shock. "Everything," he said.

When Jacen finally settled down to eat, he felt uncomfortable with his usual large plateful when these people had been starving for so long. Off in the darkness he heard the strange night sounds getting louder. A low hooting and snarling from the rocks came closer. The villagers looked up in alarm.

The ferocious sound grew louder, echoing, as if it came from dozens, perhaps even hundreds of throats. Now a rustling approached through the distant, fire-ravaged hills. After a moment of rising tension, the sentries shouted an alarm.

Tenel Ka sprang to her feet and stood beside Jacen. "What is it?" she said. "Are the mountain miners attacking?"

Anja dropped back toward the *Falcon*, a startled look on her face. Lowie sniffed the air and growled. "Dear me, Master Lowbacca," Em Teedee said. "I'm certain I can't identify the species, but I do agree—those definitely sound like the voices of predators."

The sentries yelled out, "Knaars! Knaars!" The villagers who were still eating dropped their plates of precious food and scrambled back to their homes. Some grabbed sticks, others gathered prized possessions. Many wailed in panic.

"What is it?" Jacen cried. "What are knaars?"

"Monsters!" Ynos said, pivoting on his droid leg. "It sounds like an entire herd migrating from the hills. The fire must have driven them in our direction." He hung his head as villagers continued their disorganized evacuation efforts all around them. "Now the miners will have cause to rejoice. Our village will be wiped out."

"Can you not fight these monsters?" Tenel Ka said.

"For a few minutes," one of the villagers said.

"I'm going to kill five before they take me down," a brash young man said, though the look of terror on his pale face belied his brave words.

"Killing five won't even help," Ynos said. "A migration pack contains hundreds, and the fire has driven them into a frenzy."

"We can fight beside you." Tenel Ka clutched her lightsaber. "We are Jedi."

"Then you might kill five yourself. But we'll still all fall under their fangs and claws." Ynos shook his head. "We may as well fight—there's nowhere to run." He glanced over at the deadly minefields blocking their path toward the forest, their direction of escape.

Han stood up and put a protective hand on Jacen's shoulder as the sounds of hooting and howling grew louder. They heard thundering feet, claws skittering on stones. "I could take some refugees in the *Falcon*. I can't carry nearly enough, though."

Anja stood beside the boarding ramp. "I'll get my lightsaber," she said, and ducked inside.

Jacen glanced after her with a questioning look. He had thought she always wore the weapon at her belt. But that hardly mattered now. He was much more concerned about the oncoming predators.

•  •  •

Inside the back cabin where she had stashed her pack, Anja rummaged among her belongings and took out the small black carbon-freeze unit. Her fingers trembled. She had been wanting the spice so badly; now, at last, she had a perfect excuse.

Hunching over to hide what she was doing, Anja took one of the tiny black cylinders in her hand. Its coldness felt welcome against her sweaty palm. Czethros had given her only enough andris for four doses—not as many as she wanted . . . but she would have to make it last.

Looking longingly at the three remaining packages of spice, she sealed them in her pack. Then she carefully unwrapped the insulating opaque paper that surrounded the spice. The andris spice came from a newly discovered vein on Kessel, the highest quality available.

Anja could barely wait. Outside she heard shouts, human voices among the predatory growls. She would have to hurry.

Before the spice could warm to air temperature, she slipped it under her tongue and felt the energy course through her. Her muscles sang. Her nerves became much more sensitive. Her thoughts whirled. Her blood pumped more freely, the air tasted sweeter, and her mind opened to things around her that she had never before noticed.

The spice heightened her senses, increased her

ability to fight, improved her reflexes. Anja clasped the ancient lightsaber at her side. With the full dose of spice surging through her body, she felt vibrant, powerful, ready to take on any foe.

As Han Solo led a group of escaping villagers into the *Falcon*, Anja pushed past him to run outside. At this moment she didn't care how many knaars were attacking. She could handle them all.


"There's no time to argue, Dad," Jaina said, standing at the base of the ramp as Han Solo tried to cram a last few people aboard. Zekk had already gone into the cockpit and was powering up the engines for immediate takeoff. A dozen of the remaining villagers huddled around Jaina in terror, holding sticks and agricultural implements. One woman had a small laser drilling tool.

"Take Anakin and go," Jaina insisted. "We have our lightsabers, and we have to help these people."

"But I can't leave my own kids behind," Han said, obviously torn.

"We're Jedi Knights, Dad. We have a better chance than any of these villagers. We've got to protect them."

And with that, the first knaars charged out of the darkness at the ramshackle line of buildings, looking for prey. Jaina stood startled for a moment. Tenel Ka, Lowie, and Jacen all stared at their new enemy.

"We're doomed," Em Teedee wailed.

The knaars were fast-moving reptilian predators, sleek saurians with purplish-blue scales and a silver frill of razor-sharp spines along their backs. Tails slashed back and forth, inflicting damage on anything around them with their wicked barbs. The creatures' muscular arms ended in a fistful of claws, and their immense jaws were heavy machinery designed only for eating.

The pack of bloodthirsty beasts stampeded into the village. They swiveled their heads from side to side, clenching and unclenching their grasping claws, looking for flesh to tear.

As the *Falcon* blasted its repulsorjets and rose up, Jaina watched it swivel around and fly low to the ground, approaching the predatory knaars. Han and Zekk would use blaster cannons to shoot the creatures, Jaina knew, but as the pack of monsters continued to flow from the hills, she realized it would never be enough. This migratory pack consisted of hundreds upon hundreds of members, each hungry from its long charge through the rocky hills.

Jaina's lightsaber blazed violet in her hand, and her friends drew their weapons as well. Anja rushed up, looking flushed and full of adrenaline; she danced from foot to foot, as if anxious to attack anything that came close. But the moment the knaars fell upon the nearest guard and tore the old woman apart, the other villagers turned and fled, forgetting to put up even a pretense of a fight.

Instantly Jaina saw that the battle was hopeless. Even with their lightsabers, even with the *Millennium Falcon*'s blasters, they couldn't possibly drive the knaars away. Their best choice was to flee and hope to find a place of refuge or a protected area in which they could make a stand.

And their only path to escape lay through the detonator-salted fields.

The *Falcon* blasted two of the leading knaars. Several of their fellows fell upon the bodies, stripping the meat off the bones of the dead predators. But scores of knaars kept coming.

The *Falcon* fired again. Heedless of this minor interruption, the monsters surged forward, slashing with claws, snapping their jaws at their helpless prey. Jaina, with her companions and the remaining villagers, turned and ran headlong into fields full of burrowing detonators.

# 14

AS THE *MILLENNIUM FALCON* took off with a roar, Zekk heard the villagers crowded in the back of the *Falcon* moan with fear. His attention, though, was focused on the sparks and flashes of light that signified lightsabers as the young Jedi Knights fought down below.

"Zekk, get into the gun well and start blasting those creatures!" Han Solo shouted.

"I hope your laser cannons are fully charged," Zekk said, climbing down into the gun well. He dropped into the chair, strapped in, and powered up the *Falcon*'s weaponry.

Han soared low to the ground, swooping back toward the ramshackle village. The reptilian predators prowled along, moving with the speed of hunger, cunning evident in their intelligent yellow eyes.

"There are so many of them!" Zekk muttered,

seeing the sinuous shapes dart forward like purplish-blue shadows. One of the creatures grabbed a young man and swallowed him in a single gulp before Zekk could aim the laser cannons. He wondered if that victim had been one of the brash young men who had tried to act so brave when the knaars were first coming.

Zekk targeted and fired, blowing the reptilian creature to sizzling bits. He rotated in the gun well again, seeking another target. It was difficult to zero in on the dark shadowy monsters—and he didn't dare risk hitting one of the people.

Below, a knaar advanced along the pale wall of a building. One villager had tried to take shelter around the corner, in the doorway. The knaar approached, sniffing, its claws extended. Zekk targeted and fired. The frightened villager scrambled to one side as the smoking body of the enormous reptile slumped to the ground in front of him, its fanged mouth open wide.

A shot now fired from the other gun well, striking one of the saurians in its lower leg. The moment it collapsed, honking and howling in pain, other knaars fell upon their wounded companion.

"Hope you don't mind, Zekk," Anakin said through the comm system. "I've had a bit of target training myself, but the twins get to practice more often."

The knaars continued to sweep forward. Two new ones seemed to appear for every one Zekk blasted.

Han Solo circled around and came back for another run. His concerned voice came over the comm system. "What's she doing?"

"Jaina's leading them toward the minefield!" Anakin's voice replied.

Zekk looked down and saw by the glow of the lightsaber blades that the young Jedi Knights had turned and headed with the remaining villagers into the barren fields that were full of burrowing detonators.

He thought of Jaina down there fighting against monsters and running into even more dangerous territory. His heart sank, but he gritted his teeth and grabbed the firing controls. If he couldn't pull off a spectacular rescue, at least he'd do his part to keep her safe—or as safe as she could possibly be under the circumstances.

Jaina planted her feet firmly on the rough ground and held her lightsaber high. The slavering knaar in front of her did not seem at all intimidated by her violet Jedi blade. The reptilian creature gave a high-pitched bellow, then reached forward with its claws, snapping with powerful jaws that looked strong enough to rip a repulsorpod from a starship engine.

Jaina swung forward and down with her crackling lightsaber, cleaving the monster from its shoulder down to the center of its rib cage. The creature thrashed and fell down as smoking blood bubbled from its dying heart.

Anja continued to let out loud whoops and shouts of challenge. She ran faster than the knaars, darting from one to another, wounding them with her lightsaber and diving out of the way as their claws slashed at her. She let the other carnivores do the rest of the work for her. She needed only to wound a beast, then the other knaars would tear it to pieces for the meat.

Anja's hair flew in the wind, barely held in place by the leather band. Sweat dripped down her temples onto her flushed face, but she was so full of adrenaline she seemed incapable of slowing down.

Lowbacca let out a loud Wookiee roar as he and Jacen motioned the villagers to follow them into the treacherous cropland. The villagers dropped their farming implements and ran. Panicked, some of them dashed right past the young Jedi.

"Wait! We have to find a safe path for you!" Jacen yelled. But one middle-aged woman clutching a satchel of valuables over her shoulder tore ahead in blind terror as she fled from the knaars.

"No! Wait!"

She ran through the uncleared cropland. Jacen felt an intuitive stab and a chill at the back of his neck— a premonition—just before she stepped down on one of the hidden burrowing detonators. The explosion ripped the night with a flash of brilliance and a boom of echoing thunder. The woman fell instantly, but the monsters charged toward the fields and Jacen could not take a moment to determine whether or not she had survived. The villagers screamed in despair, caught between their fear of the minefield ahead and the rampaging predators behind.

Lowie roared something at Jacen about the Force and gestured to the ground. Em Teedee quickly translated. "Master Lowbacca suggests that by using your Jedi senses, you could perhaps determine the locations of the burrowing detonators and thus avoid them. That would give us the best chance of survival."

Jacen realized that his Wookiee friend was right. If he could calm himself enough to use the Force, he might be able to map out a safe path that the villagers could follow—a path that the knaars would not understand.

"And I do suggest you be careful," the little droid added. "I have no desire to become a useless lump of floating metal with no one to translate for."

As his eyes adjusted to a darkness lit only by the green glow of his lightsaber and Em Teedee's optical sensors, Jacen trotted ahead as fast as he dared, keeping his eyes to the ground. Stretching out his free hand before him, he sensed ripples in the dirt, tiny echoes of movement—and then he spotted a slight trembling where the mechanical explosives had tunneled beneath the surface. Across the fields he could see a checkerboard pattern of places to avoid, and places where it was safe to walk.

"Follow us!" he shouted, holding his emerald lightsaber like a beacon overhead. "We can see a path!"

The ginger-furred Wookiee bellowed a confirmation, raised his own molten-bronze blade, and sprinted ahead on his long legs. A magenta glow from Tenel Ka's rancor-tooth lightsaber indicated another safe path.

Jaina and Anja remained behind to guard the group's retreat and to slow down the charging beasts. Overhead, the *Millennium Falcon*'s engines rumbled in the air. Laser beams lanced out from both gun turrets, striking knaars. Still more of the migratory pack surged like a carnivorous flood out of the rocky hills.

The villagers ran onward, grasping at any shred of hope as they followed Jacen and Lowie through the minefield. Fortunately, the knaars did not understand the explosives. They surged forward on their scaly, muscular legs, ready to snatch anyone who fell behind.

Two of the largest knaars, their silvery razor frills raised and yellow eyes glowing like lamps in the darkness, circled around to the left to charge ahead of the fleeing group and cut off their retreat. Tenel Ka turned to face them, glaring with her granite-gray eyes as if daring them to approach.

The two reptiles kept moving, staying close together. When the larger knaar stomped on one of the burrowing detonators, the explosion knocked both creatures aside, tearing open their rib cages. They lay wounded on the ground, honking and roaring in pain. Tenel Ka would have dispatched them herself, but their noises only served to attract other hungry knaars. Before long, under the double moonlight of Anobis, the two predators fell silent as their roars were replaced by the wet sounds of tearing meat and gnashing fangs.

The *Falcon* soared above the knaars, blasting more of the creatures. One of the villagers tripped. Before he could scramble to his feet again, two monsters fell upon him. When another young man turned back with a shout and tried to defend his friend, the knaars attacked him as well.

At the last instant, when it seemed the young man was surely doomed, Anja appeared beside him. Her lightsaber swept out in a blazing swath of acid yellow to lop off both forearms of the predator. The sizzling stumps of its clawed hands fell to the ground, and the monster roared, flailing about, unable to grasp anything. In blind rage it chomped at the nearest creature—another knaar. The two reptiles tore at each other, wrestling one another to the ground. In moments, other predators came in to finish off both of them.

The cropland stretched ahead, seemingly forever.

Jacen continued to run, finding it easier to pick his way around the burrowing detonators now. He saw some active ones shifting their positions underneath the soil.

Beyond, the thick forest looked like a goal line. If only they could get to the shelter of the trees, perhaps they could fight better than out in the open. But Jacen couldn't be sure. For now they were just running. He couldn't imagine how the group could possibly turn aside all the knaars, even with five active lightsaber blades and assistance from the *Millennium Falcon*.

Two more explosions ripped the night, and Jacen was relieved to see that it was only more reptilian predators stumbling upon the explosives. He looked to one side and saw a bobbing metallic sphere. Em Teedee had detached himself from Lowie's belt and drifted ahead on his microrepulsorjets, flitting from side to side in front of the beasts like a remote practice drone.

One of the largest knaars lumbered forward, attracted by Lowie's molten-bronze lightsaber blade. The Wookiee stopped his headlong run and whirled to face the monster. The knaar charged forward, exposing its razor teeth.

Em Teedee flitted in front of the monster's jaws, distracting the creature so that it snapped at the silvery sphere and diverted its fiery gaze from Lowbacca. Lowie used the moment of distraction to strike sideways, severing the knaar's body at the waist; its head still twisted and snapped even though it had no body to move.

The surviving villagers kept running. Ahead of them, the forests loomed taller. Dozens and dozens of the saurian giants had been killed, but though the pack seemed to be thinning a bit, Jacen did not feel at all relieved. The *Falcon* circled by again, blasting away.

More of the monsters died. The people continued to stumble along on the haphazard path the young Jedi Knights picked for them through the booby-trapped field. Many villagers were in shock, just following, placing one foot in front of another, unable to fully face their peril.

Jacen sensed their fear and could only hope the situation would change once they entered the thick trees. "Hurry up. Get to the forest!" he shouted. With despairing sighs, the people nearest him tried to increase their pace, but they were too exhausted. Weak from malnutrition and years of living in fear for their lives, several of them stumbled and fell, only to be helped to their feet by their equally exhausted companions. Jacen could tell that everyone's energy reserves were running out.

If they had to continue this battle, they would not make it much farther.

# 15

THE *FALCON* SWEPT overhead, strafing the on-coming monsters. Jaina and Anja fought behind the others, attacking more of the knaars. The air was filled with the snarls of the predators, the sizzling buzz of the lightsabers, and the despairing cries of the staggering villagers.

Then, to Jacen's surprise, the migratory knaars faltered in their advance, honking at each other uneasily. Many in the pack were covered with blood from their victims, both human and reptilian. But they all paused in their tracks as if unwilling to come any closer to the forest.

Jacen, sensing the monsters' hesitation, desperately tried to use his Jedi senses in another way. The knaars were at the edge of their territorial range. Jacen could feel that they had never come this far before, that the forests ahead were a great unknown, and that the predators had little desire to keep following. He sent out his thoughts, giving the knaars a vague feeling that they had come far enough, that they should turn and go home.

They smelled the blood in the air, dimly understood that a great many of their number had already died on this trek.

The knaars honked at each other in a rudimentary form of communication. With sagging shoulders and trembling knees, the villagers turned to watch in shock as the predators ground to a halt, snapping sharp teeth into the air as if they had reached some invisible boundary.

Lowie gestured with his big hairy arms to keep the people moving toward the forest during this unexpected respite. "Dear me! How very odd! I *do* hope the knaars don't change their minds and attack again," Em Teedee said.

The *Falcon* circled back and blasted one motionless knaar who stood in the lead. The other reptiles howled and snapped their jaws in defiance of the disk-shaped ship that cruised overhead. Then they turned about, moving much slower now, and began their trek back through the minefield. The stragglers stopped to snort among the scraps of meat that remained on the carcasses they'd left behind during their chase after the fleeing villagers.

Jacen stood at the edge of the forest, surveying the tall dark trees and the shadows beyond. Farther in the distance, beyond the forest, steep mountains

with winding switchback roads led up to the open
tunnels and cliffside stone villages of the miners.

The *Falcon* came to the edge of the forest and
hovered low. Jacen and Lowie reached out with
their Jedi senses, found an area clear of the burrowing detonators, and gestured for Han to land. With a
hiss not unlike that of the monstrous knaars, the ship
settled down on the uneven terrain. The boarding
ramp extended, and Han and Zekk bounded out.

"You kids okay?" Han said, breathless.

"We are, Dad," Jacen said. His sister, looking
exhausted, came up next to him.

"We lost quite a few of the villagers," Jaina said,
"but there was nothing more we could do. We tried
our best."

Zekk turned his emerald-green gaze on her. "Without you, they would all have been slaughtered. I just
wish I'd had my own lightsaber so I could have
fought at your side."

Jaina touched his arm. "You'll have one soon,
Zekk—and you'll earn it the right way."

"You helped us out just fine in the *Falcon*,"
Anakin said.

Jaina smiled. "You weren't so bad yourself—for
a little brother, or course."

Anja joined them now, sweating, flushed, but
seething with energy. To Jacen it almost seemed as
if she wanted the knaars to attack again, just so she
could enjoy the fight.

His droid foot clanging on the boarding ramp, Ynos stepped to the opening of the ship and gazed back across the fields to where an explosion boomed in the distance. One of the retreating knaars had stepped on another burrowing detonator.

"That's one way to clear a minefield," Jacen said. Anja chuckled, but Jacen didn't feel like making any more attempts at humor.

"Now we have nothing." Ynos shook his shaggy head, and his broad shoulders appeared to carry more weight than even his once-great muscles could bear. "We've abandoned our village, and the only way to get back is to cross the land-mine field again. Even then, the knaars have destroyed many of our homes, and will be waiting for us if we return to the village now. We've survived this night, but now what do we do?"

Anja stood, flushed, her lightsaber still in hand. Though the other young Jedi Knights had switched theirs off, she kept hers powered on and throbbing. Its garish yellow light threw stark shadows on her face as she pointed it up at the mountains just visible above the trees. "You can go there. That's where I used to live, my village in the mountains."

The farmers cried out in anger, and Ynos glowered at her. "What, and become slaves to the miners?"

Han Solo, perhaps still hoping to make peace between himself and Anja, came forward. "I can

take some of you up to that village in the *Falcon*.
We'll talk to their leader. I need to hear both sides of
the story anyway. This could be the best way to get
your groups talking."

"Hey, what are the rest of us supposed to do?"
Jacen said. "Should we just wait here and make
camp?"

"We could walk through the forest," one of the
villagers said.

Lowie growled, and Em Teedee translated. "Master Lowbacca recalls hearing about other traps and
detonators throughout the forest."

Jaina nodded. "Right. But it could be just as
dangerous to sit out here in the open—especially if
those knaars decide to come back."

"I know a safe way through," one young villager
said. "I've been into this forest many times. We just
have to be careful."

Han stood close to Anja, who pointedly took a
step from him. "We can take Ynos and the weaker
farmers and fly up to the mountains. The rest of you
follow us through the forest. It's safer than any of
the alternatives."

Tenel Ka looked sternly at the villagers, who,
though exhausted, seemed fearful of going to the
mountains. "If this war is to end, many things must
change. You must face your fears and be responsible
for yourselves."

"I still wish we had weapons . . . since we're

going into the household of our enemies," one of the villagers said.

"Then you'd miss the point entirely," Jaina said, still shaky and exhausted from her battle; she was growing frustrated with the villagers' stonewalling. It could well be, she mused, that the reason the civil war had dragged on for so long, and with so many innocent casualties, was that no one on either side was ready to face the challenge of making peace.

"Look," Han said, "I'm going up there even if none of you comes with me. But this is *your* war, not mine. You should be involved in this."

"We will go," Ynos said. "But I don't expect anything to come of it."

As Anja boarded the *Falcon*, Zekk turned back to Jaina. "I'll go with the ship," he said, and then looked at the villagers. "You have to have faith that there *are* options open to you. Trust in your own abilities, and in each other, and in the Force."

The villagers just mumbled. Han hugged each of his children. He looked squarely at Jacen and Jaina. "You kids are awfully brave," he said. "But it may take a while before I learn to stop thinking of you as children."

A few moments later the *Falcon* lifted off above the trees. Jacen and Jaina waved farewell, and the flattened ship's white sublight engines lit as the craft roared off across the forest toward the mountains.

Jacen, Jaina, Tenel Ka, and Lowie looked at the refugees around them.

"We're a pretty ragtag group," Jaina said.

Em Teedee drifted back down to be reattached to the Wookiee's belt. "Indeed, yes," the little droid commented.

"These people are our responsibility," Tenel Ka said. Lowie grunted his agreement and patted Jaina's back with a furry hand.

Jaina sighed. "Right. What are we waiting for?" She looked into the thick forest and gave her brother a nudge.

Jacen turned toward a young woman and two young men who claimed to know the way to the mountain village. "Let's go," he said, lifting his lightsaber like a green torch to light the way through the murk of the trees. "We've got a long march ahead of us before we get to shelter."

As the ominous animal sounds grew louder, the young Jedi Knights plunged into the thick wilderness, knowing that this forest held as many deadly pitfalls and booby traps as the minefield had.

By the time the *Falcon* flew low over the knotted mass of the forest, dawn announced its arrival with a splash of color behind the mountain crags. As the sun rose, light spilled down the rugged stone cliff faces. Zekk could make out the thin white slash of a road winding its way up the steep mountainside.

Scattered black holes marked entrances to mining tunnels and the city within the rocks.

Anja came forward from the passenger compartment and eagerly drank in the sight of the rough stone wall through the windowports. "It's been many years since I came back here," she said. "I've made my life offworld on Ord Mantell, doing whatever I could to survive."

Zekk looked at her. "Sounds familiar," he said. "I've been through a lot of the same things you have."

She glared at him. "No one's been through what I have."

"Don't be so quick to judge," he replied. His voice was hard, but it held no anger. "My parents were both killed on Ennth. When I was still young I fled offworld, and lived on the streets of Coruscant, deep in the underlevels where no one goes—at least no one who wants to stay alive. I survived for years as a scavenger, until I was kidnapped by the Shadow Academy. They trained me as a Dark Jedi to fight for the Second Imperium."

Anja shrugged one shoulder. "Our mountain villages took the side of the Empire a long time ago. It's nothing to be ashamed of."

"Maybe. But now I've learned and grown and adapted instead of wallowing in bitterness about my past. Sure, things went wrong with my life, but I think I've finally learned how to make something better."

"Or you've finally convinced yourself to let the people who hurt you get away without punishment."

The dark-haired young man could tell that Han was listening to this exchange with great interest. Zekk gave a wry smile. "If punishing other people is the most important thing in your life, then perhaps you need to look for another hobby."

Anja turned away. "Other things are important to me." Somewhat subdued, she moved to the back of the cockpit.

Ynos staggered forward and looked at the approaching mountain city. "No one from our village has gone openly into that place since the beginning of the war."

"I'd say it's about time for a change, then," Han said. He arrowed toward the widest opening in the cliffside, where lights and a landing pad were visible. Zekk guessed these must be facilities for smuggler ships, supply runners, and weapons merchants like Lilmit, who came to take advantage of the desperate plight of the people of Anobis.

Han turned to Anja. "Do we need to contact them or request permission to land?"

She shook her head. "The only ships that come in are unauthorized smugglers." She raised an eyebrow. "You know the type, Solo."

Han and Zekk landed the *Falcon* in the middle of

a broad rocky floor. Tunnels riddled the walls between buildings built from blasted-stone blocks mortared together, chips of rock cemented into multiunit structures. People came from the buildings and tunnels to study the ship suspiciously.

Anja recognized the man in front, who had a black beard, thick eyebrows, and hair with a long streak of gray down the left side. "He's the one to talk to," she said. "His name is Elis."

The miners held stone-cutting implements, pick-axes, vibrohammers, and other excavating devices. To Zekk the tools looked like potential deadly weapons.

Han extended the boarding ramp. "Let me go first. Anja, you can come with me if you like."

She looked over at him, gave a curt nod. "As long as you don't make it seem as if we're allies."

Zekk looked at the young woman, wondering what he could do to reach her and whether he could somehow dislodge the large chip on her shoulder. Anja Gallandro could have been strikingly beautiful if she hadn't had such a sour demeanor.

"Just give him a chance, Anja," Zekk said. "Nobody planned that knaar stampede, but for now we're all in this together." She shot him a resentful glare.

Han, Anja, and Zekk emerged from the ship together as the miners pressed forward. Dark-haired Elis took the lead, scrutinizing them curiously. He recognized Anja. "It's been a long time since we've seen you," he said. "And who is this you've brought with you? Another trader?"

"Han Solo," she said. "And aboard this ship are Ynos and many survivors from a knaar attack on the farming village below."

At this, Ynos hobbled forward on his droid leg. Though broad and burly, he still held the boarding ramp piston for support. The miners set up a gruff cheer.

Elis smiled, showing his teeth from within the dark nest of his beard. "Excellent work, Anja. With such important hostages, we can end this war once and for all."

"Now wait a minute!" Han cried.

Elis gestured and the miners rushed toward the *Falcon*, their stone-cutting implements raised like weapons.

# 16

IF IT HADN'T been for the minefield and the ferocious knaars behind them, the dense dark forest would not have been an acceptable option at all.

In the dim but colorful light of sunrise, Jacen could see the dense branches adorned with blue-silver leaves. Some of the trunks were smooth and metallic, others blistered with scaly orange-red bark. Lichens and mosses dangled down, clustered with lemon-yellow flowers that opened and closed in snow plant reflexes.

Tenel Ka stood next to Jacen, ready to use her lightsaber as a machete.

"Well, what are we waiting for?" Jaina asked. "Let's get hiking."

One of the young men from the village gestured ahead. "I know the way, but you'll have to follow carefully." He started forward, scanning the ground, squinting in the dim forest shadows as the ragtag band pushed their way into the wilderness.

Jacen and Jaina flanked the young villager, with Tenel Ka and Lowbacca each moving out on either side of the group, their senses alert. Lowie's dark nose snuffled the air, and his ginger fur bristled with intense concentration. The young Wookiee had survived the dangerous underlevel forests of Kashyyyk, and had won his precious fiber belt by snatching the threads from a carnivorous syren plant. Compared with the ominous forests of the Wookiee world, the woods of Anobis couldn't be too dangerous, Jacen thought.

But then, he wondered, after twenty years of civil war, how many hidden booby traps had been planted in the dense foliage?

They crunched their way along an ill-defined path. Jacen's feet popped spherical mushrooms, and wet shapeless things slithered out of the way in the weeds. With a buzzing cry of alarm, two flying creatures that looked halfway between moth and bird fluttered into the upper sparkling leaves.

Within moments it seemed as if the forest had swallowed them up, and Jacen could no longer see the cleared cropland behind them.

As the day strengthened and the sunlight grew brighter, the forest shadows remained a thick lattice around them, allowing only scattered glimpses of the bright blue sky overhead.

Tenel Ka turned her gray eyes toward Jacen; in a cold voice, she said, "Anja could have stayed here to help guide us through. Perhaps she and some of her people planted their own traps."

Jacen felt an irrational urge to defend the orphaned girl. "You don't know that about her," he said. "Just because her people have suffered as much as these"—he turned his chin toward the stumbling villagers—"doesn't mean you have to think the worst of her."

Tenel Ka gave him a puzzled look. "We just need to be aware of the dangers here," she said, and then drifted away.

Suddenly, Lowie howled and raised his hairy arms, gesturing for them all to stop. The people, already on edge, halted in their tracks, glancing around with wide eyes. Em Teedee said, "Ah, yes, Master Lowbacca. I see it too. How horrible!"

"What is it?" Jaina came close to the Wookiee. As the sunlight glittered through, Jacen could see a fine tracery stretched between the silver tree trunks, a gossamer line like the whisper of a cobweb. Lowie picked up a branch from the ground and tossed it in front of him. The branch passed through the faint lines and dropped to the ground on the other side, sliced cleanly into small pieces.

"Monofilament wire?" Jaina asked.

Jacen came close and understood the threat: a fiber so strong and so thin it surpassed even the sharpest razor blade. Anything that touched it would pass through and be sliced in two.

The villager in front stopped, looking greenish with dismay. "That wasn't here before," he said. "I slipped through here to the mountain village just six standard days ago."

"Then everything has changed," Tenel Ka said, not asking what this farmer would have been doing on his way to the mining settlement. "We must be cautious."

Carefully, they skirted the wire-strung trees, giving them a wide berth. But just as they passed into what they thought was safety, a hidden motion sensor hummed. A laser beam tracked them, spraying a red targeting lance toward the group. "Look out!" Jaina cried as the refugees scattered and dove.

The weapon discharged and blazed holes through nearby trees. One middle-aged man cried out and fell backward into the bushes with a blackened hole through one shoulder. Then, after only a few seconds, the laser ceased firing.

The young Jedi Knights waited in hiding for a few moments, expecting another attack, but when the forest fell quiet again except for the leftover squawks and rustlings of disturbed forest creatures, Jaina stood up and made her way toward the source of the laser blasts.

She found the hidden weapon, its energy pack drained. "It's a single-use munition," she said. "Strictly here to gun down one or two trespassers."

"It was made only to kill," Tenel Ka said. "To kill

anyone. Not specifically an enemy, or a friend . . . anyone."

"This is a different kind of war than anything we've seen so far," Jaina said, her expression grim. "With no objective in mind, no military targets. The factions just want to destroy everything."

"You see how horrible the miners are?" one villager said. "They plant burrowing detonators in our cropland, and look what they've done in this forest, where we have to hunt! I can't believe your father wants us to talk peace with them."

"Let's just get to the mountains and take it from there," Jacen said. "I'm sure Anja will put in a good word for us."

After encountering these two deadly traps, they proceeded with the utmost caution, and continued on for hours without further incident.

"*Not* finding any booby traps is even more nerve-racking than stumbling upon one," Jacen muttered.

Finally, after what seemed an interminable time, they paused for a rest. A few villagers had found edible fruit on a tree, which they passed around to their exhausted and hungry companions. They had been through a terrible ordeal, but over the years of civil war they had become inured to such circumstances. They walked with numb shock, fearing another trap.

Jaina and Tenel Ka suggested that Em Teedee

scan the fruit for implanted poisons, but the little droid happily pronounced each one of the red scaly clusters to be clean of contamination.

Lowie looked up at a tall, silver-trunked tree and chuffed a suggestion. "Master Lowbacca wishes to climb up to the canopy and take a look around," Em Teedee said. "He believes it might be useful in making certain we're close to the mountain village."

"I agree," Jaina said. "Go take a look around, Lowie."

With his lanky arms and legs, the Wookiee scrambled from one branch to another, in no time disappearing into the mass of silvery-blue leaves. Lowbacca loved to climb tall trees and sit in solitude. The Wookiee probably wanted to rest up there, but they couldn't sit back and wait.

With a crashing of small branches, Lowie bounded down, leaping from branch to bough, enjoying the freedom. He landed on both feet in the middle of the clearing, and gave his quick report with barks and growls.

"We are very close to the edge of the forest," Em Teedee said. "I am so pleased to be nearly out of this dismal place."

"Then let's get moving," Jacen said. "I'm anxious to have our whole group back together."

With a collective groan of weariness, the villagers struggled into motion again. The man who had been injured from the laser blast was carried along by two of his companions. They moved slowly, with exquisite care, and Jacen was very proud that they had not lost any of their party through the various traps planted among the trees.

One of the villagers called for them to move left in order to avoid a flower-filled meadow. Jacen saw nothing suspicious, though he did feel a tingling through the Force, warning him of danger. With a wan grin, the young man slipped over to another tree trunk and pushed a hidden button, switching off a tiny holographic generator. Part of the placid meadow disappeared, revealing a jagged-edged hole filled with durasteel spikes that gleamed in the forest light.

"The mountain miners aren't the only ones who can plant traps," he said proudly.

Jacen felt sickened. "That's no way to end a war," he muttered, thinking that Anja's villagers might have fallen into that deadly trap.

"You've seen what the miners have done to us," one farmer said. "How can you fault our people for defending ourselves?"

"This is no defense," Tenel Ka said.

Soon they could see daylight and cliffs through the tattered edge of the forest. The mountain and its steep pathway lay ahead.

As they were about to emerge from the forest, though, just when Jacen thought they had passed through without incident, one member of the group close to Lowbacca stepped on a flat stone, which triggered a detonator that blew up beneath one of the wide-trunked trees.

The booby trap didn't kill the woman who had triggered it, but instead blasted the roots from the huge tree and shoved it back toward them. Its sprawling branches crashed through the adjoining trees as it tumbled.

"Look out!" Jacen cried.

Lowie roared and slashed at the oncoming branches with his lightsaber. The other villagers scattered, screaming. One ran straight between two microfilament-laced trees and died an instant, bloody death. Another villager stepped on a small explosive, which blew him into the air before he fell dead and broken atop the thick-trunked tree as it crashed in among where they had all been standing only moments before.

The villagers wailed. Jacen felt a sharp pain in his heart. "We almost made it through," he said.

"We're all going to die," one of the villagers said.

"No you're not," Jaina snapped. "We just have to keep moving."

Raising her chin high, she walked bravely forward, accompanied by her brother and friends. The villagers followed, relieved to stand in the sunlight again, where they could look up at the sky after so many hours in the murky shadows. But now, free of the forest at last, they gazed at the steep pathways chiseled into the gray granite sides of the mountain, and they appeared on the verge of despair again.

"Come on. It's up this road," Jacen said. He could see the cave openings—numerous mining tunnels and the large, smooth-edged mouth where Jacen figured the mining village must be located. "My father and Ynos have already been in there, making arrangements for us. I'm sure they'll have food and water and a safe place for us all to rest."

"Or they'll just use blasters to gun us down as we walk toward them," one farmer said.

"And maybe a comet will crash down right now and wipe out the mountain village," Jaina said, impatient. "You can worry all you want, but I'd like to get where I can rest."

The started up the steep switchbacked pathway. Since it was a road used by the miners themselves, Jacen didn't expect to find any pitfalls planted there.

Though the clear sunlight baked down, the air grew thin and cooler. Overhead, wispy white clouds did little to cool off the day. The rugged mountainside provided no shade, but Jacen and his companions led the others on a slow, steady march. He could sense people watching him from above, thought he saw faces peering out from the honeycombed mine shafts in the rock face.

Now that they had accepted their destination, the villagers plodded along without complaint, without any comment whatsoever. Jacen could tell they were at the end of their rope. They had little to live for, and little hope that anything would get better soon.

Finally, panting and sweating, Jacen and his sister arrived at the top edge of the cliff city. Wearily, with a heavy arm, he gestured down to the group that had straggled out along the steep path. "Come on. It's cool, and there's shade up here."

The city seemed quiet, though he could see people in doorways, watching them suspiciously. But he could think only about getting inside and resting. The farmers trudged in, standing in the cool rock grotto, where burn marks on the floor showed that many spacecraft had come and gone.

Jacen's heart surged when he saw the *Millennium Falcon*, landed off to one side with a rippling rock wall arcing overhead. "See? We're all safe now," he said as Tenel Ka and Lowbacca brought up the rear.

"Oh, my. This is much better," Em Teedee quipped.

Then, when all the villagers stood inside the cave, the miners marched out in a well-coordinated group. Others poured out of the mining tunnels below and came up from the rear, encircling them. Jacen saw no sign of his father or Anja, nor did he see any welcoming expression on the miners' faces. Each one of them bore a weapon of some sort.

"As enemies of the mining community," one man spoke up, "we will hold you as prisoners for crimes you have committed against our people."

# 17

ZEKK FOUND HIMSELF imprisoned in the same stone-walled room with Han and Anakin Solo. The miners provided them with some sparse comforts—food and water, blankets and furniture. Anja's work, perhaps? Zekk wondered. Zekk guessed they were being treated far better than the other captive villagers, though their repeated questions about Ynos and the farmers went unanswered.

After hours without explanations, the dark-haired and bearded leader Elis came to them with surprise guests in tow, surrounded by guards from the mountain villages.

"Jaina!" Zekk cried. Jacen, Tenel Ka, and Low-bacca also came with them.

Han Solo leapt to his feet to see his children safely arrived. "You made it through the forest then," Han said. "I was worried about you."

"Had a pretty unpleasant welcoming committee

when we got up here to the mining settlements, though," Jaina said. "What do these people think they're doing?"

"They think they can end their war this way," Zekk mumbled.

"You don't understand the type of people we're dealing with," Elis said, his voice a low growl. "The farmers have done heinous things—"

"But those people were under *my* protection," Han insisted. "I'm from the New Republic. I trusted you to recognize my diplomatic immunity."

"And we are not harming you or your close friends, General Solo," Elis said. "You personally have caused us no damage. Ynos and his murderous farmers have done us great harm, though, and we will not treat them like visiting royalty." A storm seemed to pass across Elis's face, but he brought his emotions under control. "It was only out of courtesy and respect for your position that we did not execute every one of those villagers as they arrived."

"That's something at least," Han said, considering Elis through narrowed eyes.

"We've seen the cropland where you planted all those burrowing detonators. Those weapons take their toll on innocent people, as well as fighters," Jaina said. "I'd call that an act of terrorism, not a brave military strike."

"There are no innocents in the farming villages," Elis said. "I don't know what lies they've told you.

Ynos tries to make himself appear helpless and pitiable, but he has the blood of hundreds of miners on his hands."

"Ah. Aha. Yet he himself stepped on one of *your* burrowing detonators," Tenel Ka said coldly. "That is how he lost his leg."

"His heart was dead long before that," Elis answered. "For many years we had a booming business here. My mountain workers labored hard to excavate the various ores and crystals from the rich mineral veins. We still sell whatever we find to offworld traders, smugglers, anyone brave enough to come to this world and take the meager riches we have to offer. In exchange, they bring us supplies and equipment and food."

"And weapons, too," Zekk pointed out. "We stopped one of those shipments."

"We must protect ourselves," Elis answered, standing at the doorway to the stone chambers. "We have a right to do that, don't we? The farmers won't trade with us anymore. We would starve if it weren't for the smugglers. The farmers once provided us with what we needed, and we did the same for them.

"But because the bloodthirsty rebellion brought its message here to Anobis, beyond where even the Emperor cared to look, everything came crashing down. Anobis could have remained neutral, stayed out of all the fighting, but the farmers *had* to choose a side. They stopped trading with us. I ask you, what good does politics do any of us, if we're barely managing to survive from day to day?"

He gestured for them to come with him out into the dimly lit tunnels. "Come, we have something to show you," Elis said. "You need to see this."

Han went first. Zekk took Jaina's hand and followed, with the others close behind. They walked through stone corridors, excavated tunnels that jerked left and right, curving sideways and down as the miners followed veins of precious minerals. As the miners worked the mountains, it looked as though they left open chambers where new families built houses into the sides of the rough walls using rubble and tailings from the mine mortared together.

Finally the group reached a place where temporary support beams were hammered into place. Sealant foam had been sprayed on the ceilings and walls, and crossbeams stretched from one side of the tunnel to the other. Past several posted DANGER signs, Zekk could see that glowlamps had been crushed and the ceiling had fallen down in broken slabs. The debris was pale and fresh, and the air smelled dusty. Zekk heard tiny pebbles trickling down as the rockfall settled.

Elis gestured with a broad grimy hand. His fingernails were broken, as if he did most of his work by grasping the rock with his bare fingers. "This was one of our largest mining chambers, our most active vein. Numerous tunnels led to this place—and now what do you see?"

"Just rubble," Zekk said.

"You don't want to see what's buried in that rubble," Elis said, his voice hollow. "An entire mining crew was in there. Sixteen men and women, working hard at excavating. There are many tunnels like this. . . ."

"Was it a rock slide?" Jaina asked.

"No. The farming villagers did this," Elis said. "Commandos come in the night. They make their way through the forest, wait for sundown, then race up the pathway and into our mine access shafts. Their sonic punchers are quite effective. They slip them inside active tunnels, hiding them in the shadows behind stones or at floor level in cracks in the rocks where no one can see them. Then they set an activation timer and flee back into the night like the cowards they are."

"What are sonic punchers?" Jacen asked.

"Motion-activated grenades," Elis said, his lips curling, his teeth pressed so tightly together that Zekk thought they might crack at any moment. "It's not enough for the farming villagers just to destroy our tunnels or hinder our work. These weapons are more insidious than that. A sonic puncher waits until someone comes by. When it explodes, a person gets killed. Every time."

He nodded toward the rubble pile; faint pale dust

sifted into his dark hair. "As a fresh mining crew entered this grotto, their movements set off one of the sonic punchers. The trigger could have been the sound of their laughter, or the songs they sang as they went to work.

"The sonic blast cracked and shattered the rock walls and the ceiling. The entire crew was buried— crushed and battered to death under the collapse of the cave.

"We can never go into this area again. It's too unstable. We do not even dare to excavate the grotto to retrieve their bodies." Elis drew a long shuddering breath. "The miners must rest here, buried in the tunnels where they worked. Over the ages they will become part of the mountain themselves.

"Perhaps by then, there will be an end to this war." The mining leader's voice was bleak.

Seeing the anger in the man's eyes, Zekk wondered.

**18**

WHEN ALL THE prisoners, including Han Solo and the young Jedi Knights, had been separated by Elis and the miners, Anja slipped away. She saw an opportunity too good to ignore. She also knew exactly the person who could best take advantage of the circumstances.

Protas, the younger brother of the mining leader, was a bitter and grim-faced youth, barely nineteen. He had a wispy, pale beard and dusty skin from spending most of his life inside the stone tunnels, working his fingers until they bled among the rocks. But the intense young man also made frequent unofficial excursions down to the forests and croplands, where he planted traps to do his part in the fight against the farming villagers.

Now, with Anja's help, he could strike a blow the farmers would never forget.

When one of the mining crews took a break, Anja

trotted down through the tunnels asking questions until she was finally directed to Elis's younger brother. She gestured for him to join her in one of the shadowed rocky alcoves. "Protas, I need to speak to you."

He raised his eyebrows. They had been children together, and if Anja had stayed on Anobis, they might well have gotten married. But she had slipped off to Ord Mantell to join some band of smugglers. Because of their past, though, Anja knew Protas would listen to what she had to say.

"We now hold all of the farmers from one village captive inside the tunnels," she said.

Protas grinned. "I know. What more could we ask for? You led them right to us. Thank you, Anja."

"I'll tell you what more you could ask for." Anja smiled, moving closer to him. The skin under her leather headband itched, but she ignored it. Her voice was breathless as she spilled out her plan. "Their village is abandoned now. They left it completely unoccupied. We can go there tonight, slip in and burn everything down. Not only have we captured them, we can destroy everything they hold dear."

Protas's eyes gleamed, and he placed a conspiratorial hand on her shoulder. "We still have plenty of burrowing detonators, but we could never before get close enough to plant them right in the village. But now, we can rig explosives in all of their homes, make it so that the farmers destroy their own dwellings. Just by going home, they'll bring about their own doom!"

Anja's large, dark eyes twinkled. "That's even better. This way, if any of the farmers survive, they can blame Han Solo and his companions for meddling. I knew I could count on you."

Protas nodded to her. "I'll get the weapons and bring some of my men. We'll depart as soon as the sun sets."

They did not share their plan with Elis or any of the other miners. Anja, Protas, and four angry-faced commandos slipped out through one of the smaller tunnels, walking with sure feet on the smooth stone walkways. Outside, careful but confident, they dashed down the mountain switchbacks, listening to loose rocks clatter behind them as they raced along. The double moonlight provided but a pale silvery illumination and stole all colors from the landscape, marking the terrain with only lightness and shadow.

As they entered the thick forest, the sounds of night insects and small creatures rustling through the branches did not bother Anja. She had her lightsaber. And minutes before leaving the mountain village, she had gone alone into the *Millennium Falcon* and taken one of her precious doses of andris. With enhanced senses, she could experience the sharp edges of details around her. She would spot any traps waiting for them. Protas and his fighters had chosen a safe trail that avoided all of the deadly surprises they had themselves rigged.

Heading east, she wondered about the knaars that had swept through the ramshackle village and across the croplands. But that had been a full day and a half before; given slim pickings, the migratory herd's surviving members would have gone in search of other villages or abandoned livestock left to graze by farmers who had been killed during the long civil war.

The group of commandos picked their way across the barren fields. Protas consulted a diagram of where they had planted burrowing detonators. The tunneling robotic explosives could move about, but only within a certain radius of where they had been buried.

As she trotted along beside the young man, Anja saw blasted craters where detonators had exploded, some triggered by the heavy footsteps of the knaars, others by farmers bumbling into the wrong place.

The stark moonlight shone down, making the croplands look like a moonscape. None of the once-rich fields had been planted for many years. Perhaps, she thought, the miners could use their new captives as slaves to work the land again and provide food for the mountain villages. Or maybe that was just too much trouble.

She saw a shattered skeleton lying on the dirt, a

femur and a hipbone, part of a rib cage. The knaars had stripped all the flesh from the bones of their victims, whether human or reptilian. Anja felt a small twinge of pity. Han Solo and his young companions had landed the *Falcon* here despite her protests. Though reluctant, she had eaten a meal with these people, had listened to their pathetic sob story of all the trials they'd endured.

The knaars were not part of this war. They had not been sent by the mountain miners, but were simply a vicious vagary of the natural world. Anja was glad the attack had happened here, rather than in her own village. The knaars had unwittingly helped the miners' fight, removing some of their enemies.

When they reached the abandoned village, she could see the silhouettes of the dark, leaning houses, uninhabited now that the farmers had fled. Their usually well-guarded homes now had no defenses whatsoever. If the miners had come at any other time, the farmers would have put up a fierce resistance—but not this night.

"The village is ours," Protas said. "Nothing can stop us from destroying everything." The men gave a husky cheer.

They opened their packs to remove the burrowing detonators. Anja's fingers tingled in an afterwash of spice. She reached into her sack and took out one of the small mechanical bombs. It was an oblong hemisphere, segmented and flexible like a pillbug. Claws and scoops moved on articulated joints so the device could tunnel beneath the soft dirt, implant itself, and wait for an unsuspecting footstep.

With a smile, Anja decided that she would plant one of the detonators directly on the doorstep of Ynos, the village leader. She could claim that small victory for herself . . . if the one-legged farmer ever managed to get free of his captivity in the mines.

Anja bent down, cradling the device. She peered into the hollow shell of the home where Ynos lived. The hut was windowless, its walls patched and repaired. A slight evening breeze whispered through, like the breath of a sleeping man in the midst of a nightmare. She had not seen him with a wife or any family. Maybe they had died in earlier battles. The place seemed so lonely, so empty, so . . . sad.

Anja shook her head, gritting her teeth until her jaw hurt. She couldn't think of things like that now. They had a mission to accomplish.

She pushed the activation button and set the small burrower on the ground. Its metallic joints whirred, digging in. The blunt nose of the roving mine tunneled underneath the surface like a robotic mole and covered itself, shifting the topsoil so that it left no sign of its presence.

She backed away carefully, knowing that the land

mine now lay in wait for Ynos when he came back to cross the threshold of his abandoned home.

Satisfied, she jogged to a new building and planted her second detonator. Then she circled behind the scattered village and found one of Protas's men inspecting the nearly empty grain storage warehouse. He stepped toward the silo, igniter in hand, ready to set fire to the building. He looked at Anja, his eyes gleaming. "I want to see something burn this night."

"Fine," she said, "but take the grain out first. Our own villagers need it. We'll take turns carrying it back to the mines."

The young man nodded, went into the silo, and salvaged all that he found: three limp sacks containing barely enough for a single meal, though the farmers had hoarded it as if it were gold. Then Anja stood back to watch as the man set his thermal igniter in one of the corners. The flame blazed white-hot, and the silo caught fire immediately. Flames trickled up the walls to the rooftop, and soon the entire structure was engulfed.

The fire crackled and hissed, and the smoke smelled sharp and satisfying in Anja's nostrils. The other commandos shouted that they were finished, and Anja came back around to the front of the cluster of dwellings.

"Let's go," she said. "We have to get back before daybreak."

"Wait," Protas said. "I've got one last burrower to plant." He held it high, grinning through his wispy blond beard. Then, to Anja's horror, he ran straight toward the village leader's house. "I'm going to give Ynos a real surprise if ever he comes home."

"No!" she shouted. "Wait, I already—" But before he could stop, Protas stepped directly on the spot where Anja had planted her detonator.

The explosion ripped the night, throwing Protas high in the air, his clothes in flames, his body mangled. The front walls of Ynos's house collapsed into rubble. The young man's scream was swallowed in the echoes of the blast.

Anja pressed her hands to her mouth in horror. The other young men stood in shock, staring at where the young brother of their village leader had been only moments before. As rocks, clods of dirt, and other debris began to patter down like a small meteor storm, Anja suddenly broke through her stunned immobility and raced forward.

"Protas!" she shouted, knowing in the pit of her stomach that there was nothing she could do. She found the young man's body lying broken and bent in odd places, as if someone had folded him up and swatted him like a bothersome insect. His skin was burned, his open wounds bled, but his heart no longer pumped. Breath no longer filled his lungs.

She looked up in bleak despair, her dark eyes burning as she blinked and blinked. Her throat

constricted painfully. Heedless of the blood that
stained her hands, she touched the young man's
shoulder, ran her fingers along the wispy blond
strands of his beard that now would never grow to
bushy fullness like his older brother's.

The commandos stared speechless at what they
had inadvertently done. Anja's heart felt like a lead
weight in her chest. She knew that she herself, and
no one else, would have to tell Elis.

## 19

IN ONE OF the stone-walled gathering rooms, Elis's anguished wails echoed from the rocks and seemed to hang in the air like cold icicles.

Jacen shuddered at hearing the pain and sadness in that voice. The dark-bearded man cried out again, a wordless moan. He squeezed his eyes shut, and tears coursed down through the rugged crevices in his dusty face. When he ground his teeth together, his bushy beard stood out like black spines.

Jacen stood without moving, frozen in the moment next to his friends and his father. It was early morning. They had slept uncomfortably, restlessly, and then they had been summoned from their rooms to meet with the mining leader. Elis wanted to discuss what the New Republic could possibly do to improve the situation on Anobis.

With fresh hope, the group had trooped into the room to listen to the village leader and to offer suggestions as to how the long and painful civil war might finally reach a cease-fire, so that the parties could start talking. Although nothing had changed in decades, nothing was likely to change until the miners and the farmers at least began to communicate. Then, perhaps they could learn to talk in a civilized fashion.

But before Han Solo or Elis could speak, Anja had burst into the room, her face drawn, her huge eyes even more grief-stricken than Jacen was accustomed to seeing them. She kept her trembling voice low, but Jacen understood most of the devastating news she passed to Elis. Zekk caught his breath. Lowbacca, with his sensitive Wookiee ears, listened and groaned. Em Teedee made no effort to translate. Han Solo fidgeted uncomfortably. Jacen and Jaina looked at each other.

Elis turned away from them, hiding his face. The dark-haired mining leader clenched his left hand into a fist and began pounding on the stone wall of the meeting room. His chest was racked with sobs that he tried to contain within himself. As Elis smashed his knuckles again and again against the stone, Jacen saw a growing smear of blood blossoming there.

Finally, the leader drew a deep breath and seemed to control himself. When Elis opened his eyes, the look of pure hatred behind them made Jacen turn cold. "I will kill them!" Elis roared. "Bring Ynos here now!" he shouted, and other miners scurried off to the cells to fetch the one-legged farming leader.

"Why blame him?" Zekk asked, his voice surprisingly stern. His nostrils flared. "Those farmers didn't do anything this time. From what I could hear, the fault belonged to your brother—and those who went with him."

Anja looked up in dismay, but did not argue.

Jaina spoke up. "Ynos and his villagers didn't kill Protas, did they, Anja?" she said. "It was one of your own burrowing detonators, Elis. You planted them. You seeded the fields so that no one could grow crops anymore. It was an accident caused by *your* people, with your own weapons."

"Yeah," Jacen said. "You certainly can't be angry with the farmers for this."

"The true casualties of war are rarely those we expect," Tenel Ka added.

Stricken, Elis was unable to sort through his thoughts. He didn't seem to hear anything the young Jedi Knights said. He stood up and looked down at his bloodied knuckles, as if surprised. "I will call Lilmit or one of our other suppliers. They will help us get enough weapons to wipe out the farmers and end this war forever. My brother will be the last casualty on our side."

"It's kind of odd, don't you think?" Han Solo said. "That Lilmit is selling weapons to both sides,

I mean. If you buy more, then the other side will buy more. Pretty soon you won't be able to count all the victims."

"What?" Elis said, astonished. "Lilmit? Impossible. He wants to help *us* win."

"No," Anja croaked, her voice rough and weak. "We intercepted him on his way here and confiscated his cargo. He had weapons for our miners, all right. But he also had sonic punchers and other equipment the farmers use against us."

"They're selling to *both* sides?" Elis said in horror.

Just then, the guards dragged in an indignant and weary-looking Ynos. His mechanical droid leg scraped along the stone floors. He had heard the last of the exchange. Standing, he shook off the grasp of the guards.

"You buy weapons from Lilmit as well?" he growled.

Elis looked at him, and the expression on his face rippled with pure rage. "They're playing both sides for fools—supplying all of us, while we continue to fight and harm each other all for nothing!"

"I wouldn't be so sure." Zekk crossed his arms over his chest. "They may have been keeping this little war going for as long as possible, just because business is so good."

Ynos and Elis glared daggers at each other.

"I understand your little brother was trying to

destroy our village, and had a little accident," the one-legged man taunted.

With a roar, Elis charged toward the farming leader, but Jacen and Jaina moved with their father and friends to block his way.

"Protas shouldn't have gone to the village last night. Anja was there with him," Jaina said. "Ynos had nothing to do with it."

"It's my fault," Anja said. "I planted that burrowing detonator to destroy Ynos's home. It went off . . . too soon, and the explosion killed your brother."

"My home is gone?" Ynos said. "Our village is ruined, as well." He hung his shaggy head. He turned his eyes toward Anja. "And who would have died if the detonator hadn't gone off 'too soon'?"

Anja did not meet his eyes.

"Someone must pay," Elis insisted. "You farmers have much to atone for—all of the sonic punchers you have planted, the tunnels you have collapsed, the miners you have killed with your cowardly hidden weapons."

Ynos drew himself up. "And who will pay for all of *my* people who died while trying to plant crops for our very survival? What of the victims of your burrowing detonators, your monofilament nets in the forest?"

"Nothing you do can bring those people back," Jacen said. "Blaster bolts! If you keep trying to take revenge for what the other side does, this war will never end."

"Your people have demonstrated that over the last twenty years," Anakin pointed out.

"But we can't just forget and put it all behind us," Elis said with a scowl. "Too much blood has been shed, and too many traps remain. People will continue to die for years as they stumble upon leftover sonic punchers buried by these . . . renegades in our precious mines."

"And how are we to farm?" Ynos cried "All of our most fertile land is still full of deadly explosives. We can't even plow the fields, much less plant our seeds."

"Then maybe all of you should work together to clear out those traps and explosives," Jacen said, "instead of wasting all your time rigging more murder weapons to strike back at each other."

"Why spend your efforts on causing more damage instead of on healing your world?" Tenel Ka asked.

Anja looked up at them, her eyes weary. She heaved a huge sigh. "You ask the impossible."

Jacen and Jaina looked at each other, recalling their uncle Luke's story of his Jedi training with Yoda. Luke had thought Yoda asked the impossible.

"Believing that peace is impossible—that you *can't* change—is what keeps your war going," Jaina said.

"That's a surefire way to fail," Jacen said.

"It's true," Zekk said. A look of pain flashed in his emerald eyes. "You have to be *willing* first—willing to do things a new way, willing to look forward instead of back."

"And speaking of willing," Han said, "our offer still stands. If you're willing to forget the word 'impossible,' we're willing to help out in any way we can."

Elis closed his eyes tightly, his face etched with grief, as if he were reliving decades of murder, destruction, and hopelessness in his mind. "What do you say, old man?" he said, turning toward Ynos without opening his eyes. "Are we willing?" A single tear escaped from beneath one lid.

Ynos's voice was rough with emotion. "Our way has helped no one—except for those who sold us weapons. I do not know how we can make this change. But, yes, I am willing."

Elis opened his eyes. "Where do we begin?"

Anakin's face lit up as he considered the problem. "I think I just might have an idea."

# 20

WHEN THE YOUNG Jedi Knights began clean-up operations on Anobis, they realized it wasn't exactly the type of battle they were accustomed to fighting . . . but it was a battle nevertheless.

The nondiscriminating weapons planted by both sides had taken countless victims, and not just soldiers in battle. Many of the deadly traps had been set years, even decades before, and continued to take their toll, as much in terror as in blood.

Jacen doubted the planet's scars would ever vanish completely, but with the temporary cease-fire brought on by grief and despair, the wounds might at least begin to heal.

Han Solo came back from the *Millennium Falcon* in the landing grotto. He rubbed his hands briskly together and smiled at his children. "Well, I just sent out a message, summoned a little help from a few friends."

"We can use all the help we can get," Zekk said.

Han gave one of his famous wry smiles. "You saying a couple of Jedi Knights can't handle everything?"

Lowie stood tall among them, chuffing a suggestion. Em Teedee translated. "Master Lowbacca believes that perhaps some of the key commandos from each side could help us locate the booby traps that were planted."

"If they can remember," Jacen said. "There are so many of them."

"Then we've got a lot of work to do," Jaina observed. "What are we waiting for?"

While the others went off on separate missions, Jacen and Zekk made their way to the dangerous mining tunnels. Accompanied by Anja and two downcast farmers they searched for hidden sonic punchers.

Many times, farmers had slipped into the mining tunnels from the cliff face, and so Jacen, Zekk, and Anja, and the others climbed down the steep mountain path outside and entered through the boarded-up entrances to played-out shafts.

The moved along holding shining glowsticks that bore an eery resemblance to miniature lightsabers. The pale, cold light spilled ahead of them into the passageways. The farmers blinked, warily looking in both directions. Anja followed, tense and seething, lips pressed together, as if she could barely resist the urge to pull out her ancient lightsaber and strike these enemies down. But she contained her anger and focused on disarming the hidden traps.

"We haven't worked these tunnels for years." Anja narrowed her sad eyes at the farmers. "It would have been foolish to plant a sonic puncher here."

The two young men looked sheepishly at each other. "We don't know much about your work," one said. "We just planted the punchers wherever we could."

They turned a jagged corner to a branching of dark tunnels. The glowsticks shone ahead, but pushed back the shadows only a small distance.

"Wait," Zekk said, holding up his hand.

Jacen felt his senses tingling. "Down there," he said, pointing to the left.

One of the farmers shook his head. "No, we didn't go down there. I'm sure of it."

"Doesn't matter," Zekk said. "We sense danger down there."

"Could be an older trap," one of the men suggested.

"Old or new, we have to get rid of them all," Jacen said. "You three stay here." He and Zekk edged forward, pushing the glowsticks into the ominous tunnel.

"Quiet," Zekk cautioned in a whisper. "Sonic

punchers are activated by disturbances in the air. If we get too close, we'll set it off."

Despite their warning to stay back, Anja came up behind them. "How are you going to get rid of it? Once a puncher is activated, no one can get close without blowing it up."

"Maybe we can," Jacen murmured, raising an eyebrow. For some reason, he wanted to impress Anja. He saw sweat darkening the leather headband she wore and beading on her forehead. He and Zekk stood shoulder to shoulder, looking deeper into the darkness.

"Our Jedi senses can do the searching for us," Zekk said in a low voice. He turned to his friend. "Are you up to it?"

Jacen nodded. Calming himself, he reached out with his mind, and used the extra eyes and ears the Force gave him. He could tell Zekk was doing the same. They scanned into the dimness of the tunnel, locating rocks, crystalline formations, rubble piled at the bottom of the channel. His mind moved in farther. He breathed slowly, feeling his heartbeat. Blood pounded in his temples.

There. He sensed something wrong, an object out of place . . . a *device* that didn't belong in the rocky debris.

"Found it," Jacen said.

"Me too," Zekk answered.

With his mind Jacen ran invisible fingers over an

outer metal casing, glittering controls, and finely tuned sensors just waiting to be triggered by an unexpected motion in the air.

"Careful," Jacen whispered. "Help me lift it out."

They used the Force, stretching out together with their minds, to move the rubble gently away from the weapon. This small device contained enough power to crack open fissures in the tunnel walls and bring the entire ceiling down.

Anja came up close behind them. "Maybe you should just detonate it in there," she said. Her soft words startled Jacen, nearly making him lose· control of his concentration. He could feel her warm breath on the side of his face and neck. "Throw a few rocks down the tunnel and set it off."

Zekk glanced back over his shoulder toward her. "No. We may need to explode some of them, but I think we can do most of the punchers our way. There's been enough damage already."

Working as a team, they used a silent Jedi mind grip to lift the sonic puncher, carefully raising it off the floor. Just then, a loose rock fell from a pile and clattered to the floor. The sound was like thunder, and the vibration was enough to activate the trigger.

"No!" Jacen cried. With his mind he clamped onto the distant controls, freezing the mechanism.

Zekk reacted in a different way, lashing out with the Force to rip circuits free inside the detonator, deactivating it forcibly. An instant later his face fell, as if he was ashamed of himself. "You found a better way, Jacen."

"Either one would have worked," Jacen said. "Just let the Force guide you, and stay calm inside."

Together they walked into the tunnel and picked up the now-inert sonic grenade. Jacen handed it to Anja. "A souvenir for you. Our first success."

"Fine," she said, and looked skeptically at it. "But don't get cocky. I hear we've still got about forty to go."

Lowbacca reveled in being in the forest again, despite the hidden traps and dangers he knew waited for them there. Tenel Ka trotted at his side among the silvery trees. A few miners and farmers came with them, trying to recall where each group had planted weapons.

They stopped at the edge of a pristine-looking meadow, with its colorful wildflowers like fireworks among the grasses. Tenel Ka marched immediately to where the holographic generator covered a spike-filled pit. She picked up a rock and threw it. They all watched as it vanished into the lush grasses. The camouflage hologram rippled with a flicker of static, then returned to its serene appearance.

The miners gasped. Lowie went over to a stout tree and with his bare hands ripped the controls away, shorting them out. The hologram flickered and faded, revealing the open pit and its sharp spikes.

The miners looked furious at the thought of the cowardly trap the farm villagers had set. But one farmer snarled, "Is that any more vicious than your monofilament wire that can butcher us into pieces as we walk?"

The miners took the lead, showing where they had strung their wires between trees. Lowie could barely see the laser-sharp lines, but he knew they were there. He and Tenel Ka drew their lightsabers and swept through the air, as if fighting invisible spiderwebs. The searing blades severed the monofilament wire, making the passage safe again.

Lowie sniffed. On the forest floor below where the cutting web had been strung, he saw numerous dead animals: birds whose wings had been neatly amputated when they flew between the wrong trees, and larger forest animals, cut down as they walked, left to decay in the forest mulch, surrounded by the bodies of carrion eaters who'd also ventured into the deadly trap.

Both sides were subdued now, resentful but cowed.

"Come," Tenel Ka said gruffly, marching forward. Her pale skin and glittering lizard-hide armor looked out of place in the silent, primeval forest. "We have much ground to cover, and years of accumulated dangers to eliminate."

Jaina once again took her place as the *Millennium Falcon*'s copilot. She felt very comfortable in the position, though she realized that as soon as they left Anobis, her father would travel with Chewbacca again.

She didn't feel sad, however. Being her father's copilot was a wonderful experience and had taught her much, but she preferred flying the *Rock Dragon*. Even though the Hapan passenger cruiser technically belonged to Tenel Ka, Jaina knew that once her skills were sufficiently advanced, she would get a cruiser of her own, perhaps an old ship like Zekk's *Lightning Rod*, or maybe something newer and faster. . . . She grinned at the thought.

Han looked over at her, wondering what she was thinking. "Don't get distracted now, Jaina," he said. "This is a touchy operation."

The *Falcon* cruised over the treetops and suddenly burst out above the open cropland. Jaina could see where the land had long ago been cleared for farming. Green weeds showed how fertile the dirt could be, but first the deadly harvest planted beneath the soil, the burrowing detonators that waited for any unsuspecting footfall, would have to be removed.

"All right, kids," Han said. Anakin came forward to stand between Jaina and his father. "I need something that not even the *Falcon* can do for me. Use your Jedi senses to help your old man find those detonators and get rid of them."

Anakin nodded, squinting his eyes in concentration. Jaina recalled how she had avoided the buried explosives during their desperate flight from the knaars. In her mind she saw a dotted pattern of ripples below, like a scrambled checkerboard of targets on the ground.

"There's an awful lot of them, Dad," Jaina said.

"Swarms," Anakin added.

"Well, let's get started then. Give me some coordinates."

"Just fly in a slow zig-zag across the field, Dad," Jaina said.

"It will be hard *not* to find a detonator," Anakin agreed. He helped his sister aim one of the ship's laser cannons.

Jaina fired from the copilot's controls, and was rewarded with a large explosion, much greater than the laser should have made. "Got one!" she cried.

"There are hundreds more," Anakin said.

Jaina targeted another detonator, and the laser cannon eliminated that one as well. After she blew up three more, Han asked, "We getting close?"

"Not in the least," Jaina said. "This'll take all day."

"A single footstep could set one off at any time," Anakin said. "But they move around a bit. We'll have to target each one precisely."

"You kids are doing great." Han patted the *Falcon*'s control panel. "But I think I've got a faster way."

"We can't miss a single one," Jaina warned. "It could start the fighting all over again."

"Don't worry, I think we can get full coverage." Han activated the ship's deflector shields, which had blasted comets out of the way during their final trial run of the Derby. Now, as he cruised low, the force field pressed down, like a heavy unseen hand, on the ground. "We'll just cruise over the fields. The force field will push down and pop any of those land mines we encounter."

The *Falcon* moved slowly, its deflector shields placing pressure on the dirt. As the deflectors ruffled the soil, one of the burrowing detonators exploded directly beneath them, rocking the craft from side to side.

Jaina and Anakin looked at their father.

"Not to worry," Han said. "This ship can handle a lot more than that."

They flew in a straight line as Anakin marked the pattern of their flight on a holochart he called up. Three more detonators exploded. Clouds of suspended dust and smoke looked like phantom trees growing from the barren field.

"Ah, looks like our reinforcements have arrived," Han said.

Jaina looked into the sky to see the fleeting shape of another ship—a familiar ship. The Hapan passenger cruiser circled low, coming in to pace them. "But—we left the *Rock Dragon* on Ord Mantell."

Han shrugged. "I asked somebody to pick it up for us." He toggled the comm switch. "Hey, Kyp. That you, kid?"

"You bet," Kyp Durron said. "With Streen—and I brought some more assistants from the Jedi academy, in case you could use an extra hand."

"Or hoof," another voice broke in.

"Is that Lusa?" Jaina asked, suddenly recognizing the voice of the centaur girl who had come to Yavin 4 after escaping from the Diversity Alliance.

"Yes, we've got Lusa here, and young Raynar, another friend of yours," Kyp continued. The young man from the Bornaryn trading fleet greeted them.

"Looks like we're going to have quite a reunion tonight," Kyp said. "But for now, we've got some land mines to clear."

"Hey, I'm just a good pilot who happens to be here on a diplomatic mission," Han Solo said. "I'm trusting all of you to use your Jedi powers to make sure we do a thorough job."

The two ships parted and began to crisscross the vast acreage that had once been cropland. It was clear that the fields of Anobis could grow food enough to feed all its inhabitants, once the land was made safe again.

The rumble of repeated land-mine detonations sounded like rapid gunshots in the empty sky. The *Rock Dragon* and the *Millennium Falcon* continued without pause. Their deflector shields pushed down on the fertile ground, at the same time smoothing out many of the jagged holes and pits left from earlier explosions.

"Never thought we'd be using our spaceships to harvest bombs," Jaina said.

Han smiled at her. "The *Falcon*'s good for just about anything," he said. "'Course I prefer to give her more glamorous duties."

Both ships left their comm systems open. Jaina chattered with Raynar and the centaur girl Lusa, catching up on news as they continued their work. Toward the end of the afternoon, Lowie and Tenel Ka emerged from the dense forest and waved up at the ships crisscrossing the air.

"Looks like they're finished," Jaina said. "But I have the feeling we just did the easier parts of the job. We can go home once these weapons are cleaned up. But the people of Anobis still have to come to terms with all their hatreds and prejudices. They've got a long history to overcome."

Han looked at his daughter. Another burrowing detonator exploded behind them, but he didn't even seem to notice. "The rest is going to be up to them," he said. "Sure, your mom'll send in some New Republic peacekeepers and inspection teams, but these people have to determine in their own hearts whether this war will ever end."

## 21

"THAT WAS HARD work. I'm starved," Jaina said. She collapsed onto a wooden bench beside her brother and looked appreciatively at the feast being laid out by both miners and farmers on long shady tables in the fading afternoon sunlight at the foot of the mountains.

"*You're* hungry?" Jacen said. "Hey, what about us? Zekk and Anja and I weren't just sitting on a ship and flying around all day, you know. There was nothing between us and those explosives except for the Force and our lightsabers."

"Lowbacca and I were also in considerable danger afoot," Tenel Ka pointed out.

Jaina grinned good-naturedly. "Guess you're probably even hungrier than I am then, huh?"

The one-armed warrior girl crooked an eyebrow at her. "This is a fact."

Anja stood with feet spread apart, shook back her

long silky hair, and heaved a dramatic sigh. "I could eat a whole gundark right about now, without even bothering to cook it first."

"I know what you mean," Zekk said.

Jaina noted with amusement—and perhaps a hint of alarm—the playful look Anja directed at both Zekk and Jacen as she said, "I don't like to share."

Jacen chuckled. "Don't worry. We'll find our own gundarks."

"So, uh, how does it feel?" Jaina asked, changing the subject. She looked at Anja, then gestured toward the miners and farmers as they uneasily worked together to prepare the meal.

"Strange," Anja admitted. "It's . . . hard to start trusting someone you've hated all your life. I'm not sure what to do with myself now. I've always been a fighter and a smuggler, not a miner."

"Why not come back to Yavin 4 with us?" Jacen suggested. Jaina blinked in surprise at what her brother had said.

"Really?" Anja asked.

"Sure," Zekk said with a twinkle in his emerald eyes. "After all, you're pretty dangerous with a lightsaber already. Master Skywalker might be able to teach you a bit more about control."

Jacen said, "It's obvious you've got some talent."

A suspicious look entered Anja's enormous dark eyes. "I don't know. I don't take rejection very well.

Your Master Skywalker might not let me study there. I'd hate to make the trip for nothing."

"Trip? Where're you heading?" Han Solo asked, striding up with Anakin, Kyp Durron, and Streen.

"Um, Jacen had an idea that Anja might want to study for a while at the Jedi academy," Jaina said uncertainly.

Kyp smiled and looked at Han. "I was quite a handful myself, as I recall."

Han drew a deep breath, let it out slowly in a soundless whistle. He looked into the eyes of the young woman who had hated him for so many years. "If you're really interested, I'll put in a good word for you with Luke."

Jaina tensed, expecting Anja to throw her father's offer back in his face. Instead, the young woman said stiffly, "Thank you. I accept." Then she whirled, her long hair lashing like a silken whip behind her. "Now if you'll excuse me," she said over her shoulder. "I have to say some goodbyes. I'll return in an hour." Without another word she sprinted off toward her village.

Anakin stared quizzically after the young woman. "It's all settled then?" he asked.

"Guess so," Jaina murmured.

Just then Lusa trotted up, with Raynar running easily beside her, as if he were now used to such exercise. "Elis says the feast is almost ready," the centaur girl said. "We must come and eat."

Han nodded. "We'll stay for evening meal, and then take off. You kids want me to fly back to Yavin 4 with you?"

"Naw," Jacen said. "We'll be fine in the *Rock Dragon*."

"We can manage," Jaina added. "There's plenty of room for all of us."

Her father nodded again, as if he had expected this.

"In that case, do you mind if Streen and I get a lift back to Coruscant with you?" Kyp Durron asked. "Master Skywalker told us that's where we'd begin our next assignment."

This suggestion brought a grin of pleasure to Han Solo's face. "Hey, no problem. Be just like old times, huh, kid?"

"Two of the best hotshot pilots in the galaxy together again," Kyp agreed.

Anakin looked over at his sister. "This could be interesting."

Jaina bit her lower lip and looked in the direction Anja had taken toward the mountain village. "Yes. Very interesting."

Anja stood impatiently in front of the viewscreen in the mining village's secondary comm center. She crossed her slender arms over her chest and tried not to fidget. It would not do to show her impatience.

Why was the transmission taking so long to go through?

Finally, the static on the screen cleared, revealing the close-cropped green hair and the rugged, visored face she had been expecting: Czethros. "Things didn't go exactly as you had planned," she said with a tight smile. "Solo is still alive. But I've managed to get the situation back under control."

Czethros's image remained impassive, but Anja could see the interest in his eyes. "Tell me," he said.

"Solo's own children invited me to join them at the Jedi academy."

Czethros's mouth opened slightly. He looked suitably impressed.

"Once I'm in place on Yavin 4," Anja went on, "I'll win their confidence. And I believe many opportunities will present themselves. . . ."

Czethros nodded his moss-green head, and a dangerous smile formed on his face. "You've done well. As long as you can stay in touch with me, I'll make sure you're supplied with andris."

Czethros broke the connection and Anja allowed herself to relax. That was all she had needed to hear.

For Jacen, the return trip to Yavin 4 proved to be endlessly fascinating. While Jaina and Lowie piloted the *Rock Dragon* with Em Teedee as their navigator, Zekk, Raynar, Lusa, Tenel Ka, Anja, and Jacen gathered in the crowded crew cabin to talk.

They shared stories of their adventures on various planets. Lusa spoke of her experiences with the Diversity Alliance. Zekk talked about the Shadow Academy and about his time as a bounty hunter. Raynar spoke haltingly of the bounty Nolaa Tarkona had placed on his father's head, and of Bornan Thul's death in the Emperor's plague storehouse. Jacen and Tenel Ka explained how the warrior girl had lost her arm in a lightsaber training accident. Last, Anja shared more about her experiences growing up as an orphan on the war-torn planet of Anobis.

As she told her story, tears formed occasionally in her huge sad eyes, but she never allowed them to fall. Jacen found it hard to imagine the horror of seeing so many friends die year after year.

"We got rid of a lot of the land mines, punchers, and detonators," Jacen said, trying to comfort her. "Maybe now your people can stop living in fear."

"Ah," Tenel Ka said. "Aha. But that is only a beginning."

"That's true," Zekk said. "War changes people. They're going to have to learn how to trust and accept each other now. It . . . it doesn't come naturally."

Anja looked ruefully around at the faces of the young Jedi Knights. "That's going to be difficult for me too. It's been a long time since I trusted anyone."

Lowie roared a comment from the cockpit. "Master Lowbacca wishes to inform you that we will be emerging from hyperspace in one standard minute," Em Teedee said.

"Almost there," Jaina added. "Hang on, everybody." The companions moved forward to the cockpit to get a good view of the tiny jungle moon.

When it appeared in the front windowports, Jacen said, "There it is, Anja. Yavin 4. For now, your new home."

**Turn the page for a sneak preview of Jacen and Jaina's next adventure . . .**

STAR
YOUNG JEDI KNIGHTS
WARS ®

**Trouble on Cloud City**

Lando Calrissian offers the young Jedi Knights a rare opportunity—a vacation on Cloud City. They jump at the chance—as long as their new friend, the mysterious Anja Gallandro, can come along.

Anja is happy to be included. But little do the twins know that they are actually helping Anja hatch her sinister plan. A plan that goes far deeper than simple revenge . . .

Coming in August '98 from Berkley Jam Books!

JAINA SOLO, DAUGHTER of the legendary pilot and smuggler Han Solo, ran through the dense jungles of Yavin 4 as if her life depended upon it. Crashing sounds in the nearby underbrush bore testament to the fact that she was not alone.

Her mother, former princess of Alderaan and the New Republic's current Chief of State, would have been aghast at Jaina's disheveled appearance. Her straight brown hair dripped with sweat. Leaves, branches, and trailing vines whipped at her face, though she hardly seemed to notice.

She let the Force guide her footsteps. The rich spicy scent of jungle foliage filled her lungs. Jaina, out of breath, ran headlong through the alternating light and shadows of late afternoon.

The crashing sounds came not from pursuing enemies, however, but from her companions: the ginger-furred Wookiee Lowbacca and Tenel Ka, princess of the Hapes system and warrior from the world of Dathomir.

Still, Jaina fled—not from her friends or from the Jedi academy where she trained, but from a feeling that she couldn't shake, a sense that *something* was not right.

The feeling hounded her like a nek battle dog snapping at her heels. From far behind Lowie bellowed a suggestion, and Jaina veered off onto a narrow path that would lead them to a clearing near the river.

"Got it! Almost there," she yelled without slowing down. The unpleasant feeling still followed her like some vicious beast ready to pounce. She hurdled a Massassi tree log that had fallen across the path. Tenel Ka and Lowie converged behind her and leapt over the fallen tree. Jaina and her friends burst through the dense foliage and into the clearing by the broad, slow-moving river.

Near the water stood a boy, about Jaina's age, with a round face and spiky blond hair. Beside him was a centauriform young woman whose rich cinnamon hair matched the color of her glossy flanks. Her long mane flowed down her bare back. The two had been skipping stones on the water, but at Jaina's approach, the blond-haired young man looked up.

"Well, well, well. Glad you could make it," he said.

"Hi, Raynar, Lusa," Jaina said, coming to a stop and panting hard. "Are you all right?"

"The opportunity to exercise was most welcome," Tenel Ka said.

Lowie and his miniaturized translating droid, Em Teedee, added their greetings. Lowie combed his long fingers up through the dark streak in his wind-blown fur.

Lusa gave them a measuring look and said, "Is anything wrong?"

Jaina shrugged uncomfortably, still unable to pinpoint her feeling. Avoiding her friend's gaze, she took off her flightsuit and removed her boots.

Raynar glanced around. "Where are Jacen and Zekk? Didn't they come with you?"

Jaina sighed and waded into the river. Once in the shallows, she dug her toes into the mud and pondered. This, of course, was the heart of the problem.

"Our friends Jacen and Zekk opted to assist Anja Gallandro with her lightsaber training," Tenel Ka explained. "She already has the weapon, but wishes to become more proficient in its use."

Raynar looked disappointed. "Couldn't they have done that later?"

"It was their choice," Tenel Ka said simply, plunging into the river water without the slightest hesitation.

"They could have invited Anja along to go swimming with us," Raynar said. "It might have made her feel welcome, more at home."

At last Jaina said what was on her mind. "Anja's been at the Jedi academy for weeks now, and I don't think she'll ever feel at home. I'm not even sure she *wants* to. I've tried to be friendly and show her around, but most of the time she just ignores me—except when she wants to complain about something. Like the weather: She hates the humidity. Or the food: 'It's not prepared properly.' And our lessons: 'It's stupid to sit around thinking at rocks all day.' Not to mention the entertainment: 'There's nothing to do on Yavin 4.'"

Lowie rumbled a comment. "Indeed," Em Teedee translated. "Master Lowbacca has made every effort to befriend Anja Gallandro, but to no avail."

Tenel Ka surfaced and shook back her red-gold warrior braids. "I, too, have been rebuffed."

"She has not spoken five words to me," Lusa said.

Jaina sighed again. "She seems perfectly happy to spend time with Jacen . . . and Zekk."

"And they with her," Tenel Ka pointed out. Jaina couldn't tell whether or not she detected a note of jealousy.

Raynar opened his mouth as if he were about to ask something, then seemed to think better of it. He simply said, "Oh." The blond-haired boy looked curiously from Jaina to Tenel Ka for a moment, then added, "Well, I hope they know what they're doing." He flushed slightly. "I . . . I mean, lightsaber practice with someone who isn't really trained in the Force can be pretty dangerous."

Jaina looked up and flashed him one of the lopsided grins for which the Solos were so famous. "Zekk assured me he was just going to coach. And I don't think we need to worry about my brother. He's fought some of the most ferocious creatures alive with his lightsaber." She chuckled. "Including Tenel Ka."

"This is a fact," Tenel Ka said, putting her single hand to the rancor-tooth lightsaber hilt that hung at her waist. The warrior girl's other arm had been cut off above the elbow in a lightsaber training accident.

"Now," Jaina continued, "why don't we all swim. That *is* why we came, isn't it? Anyway, Zekk and Jacen are Jedi. I'm sure they won't let anyone get hurt."

"Ow!" Jacen yelped, pulling back with the hand that held his emerald green lightsaber. "You singed the hair off my arm!"

A bland smile was fixed on Anja Gallandro's face, a smile that did not reach her impossibly large, sad eyes. She seemed not the least bit perturbed. "Then I guess you should have moved a bit faster, huh?"

Zekk approached the two combatants. His intense green eyes flashed an emerald fire as cutting as that of

Jacen's lightsaber. "That was a foolish risk, Anja," he said. "This practice is to learn about *control* with the weapon."

Anja shook back the dark silky hair that fell to her waist, held out of her eyes only by a strip of leather bound about her forehead. She gave him a haughty look. "You're just angry because I don't need to control my fighting, and it makes you real Jedi look bad."

"No. That move was unnecessarily risky," Zekk said in a stern voice that Jacen had rarely heard him use before. "Not only did Jacen almost lose a chunk of his arm, but if *he* had been trying to hurt *you*, you left him the perfect opening to sweep back with his lightsaber like this"—he demonstrated with a stun stick he was holding—"slice through your ribs, and cut you into two neat pieces."

Anja glared at Zekk for a long moment. He endured her gaze without flinching and reached back to retie the narrow thong that kept his hair in place at the nape of his neck. A symbolic gesture, Jacen guessed—

Zekk's hair was as dark as his past, yet he had learned to control it, to put it behind him. Anja, on the other hand, spoke often with anger about her life; she barely kept her impulses in check, just as her headband barely kept her hair from flowing wild. Jacen glanced back and forth as the tension built between his two friends.

Finally Anja looked away and shrugged one shoulder. "You said yourself this was a lesson in control. I knew Jacen wouldn't take advantage of the opening."

Jacen's mouth fell open in astonishment. But before he could speak, he saw Master Luke Skywalker emerge from the base of the Great Temple and gesture for him to come over.

"I have to go talk to Uncle Luke," he said warily.

"Can you two keep working for a few minutes without me?" He offered his lightsaber to Zekk and gave a tentative grin. "Without killing each other, I mean?"

"I can manage that," Zekk said.

"Anja," Jacen warned, "just remember that you can't afford to make mistakes like that one against a *real* enemy. He won't give you a second chance."

She smiled her imperturbable smile. "Don't be so sure."

Jacen shook his head. Running a hand through his disheveled brown curls, he trotted off to where the Jedi Master stood in the shadow of the rebuilt pyramid.

"How's the training going?" Luke Skywalker asked, his eyes on Anja and Zekk as they began to spar again. Anja's acid-yellow blade swept out in a wild and furious attack, but Zekk parried her blows easily.

"She, um . . . has her own way of doing things," Jacen said. "Kinda stubborn, you know?"

"So I've noticed," Luke said. "I've spent several training sessions with her myself and—in spite of the talents you see in her—I haven't been able to sense any Jedi potential at all. She doesn't sense the Force."

"Hey, that doesn't mean it's not there," Jacen said. "Give her some time. She's had a tough life. Maybe it's just hidden somehow."

Luke pursed his lips. "Perhaps. But if it weren't for the fact that your father asked me to keep her here at the academy as a special favor, I'm not sure I'd allow her to stay. She has a deep shadow inside her."

"Well, thanks for giving her a chance," Jacen said. "I'm sure you won't be disappointed."

FOR THE THIRD time that morning, Tenel Ka replaced a cyberfuze on the *Rock Dragon* that did not need replacing. Beside her, Jaina, biting her lower lip, hunched over the navigational console of the Hapan passenger cruiser. She used Em Teedee to run an unnecessary calibration check, while Lowbacca conditioned the already clean outer hull with lubricants.

The three of them had felt inexplicably downcast, Tenel Ka thought, since the previous afternoon when Jacen and Zekk had chosen not to accompany them to the jungle. Today, the warrior girl had risen at first light from an unsatisfactory sleep and performed the most rigorous calisthenic routine she had ever devised for herself. She had hoped to purge any lingering resentment from her mind . . . but it hadn't worked.

After that, she had scaled the outside of the huge Massassi pyramid, single-armed, wearing her briefest lizard-hide and using only her grappling hook and fibercord to assist her. This exertion had proved stimulating enough that she decided to go for a ten-kilometer run as well.

Jaina, having just finished a long Jedi meditation, had

trotted up to join her. Although Jaina was fresh, she was
not as strong a runner as Tenel Ka, and the warrior girl
enjoyed the feeling that she could outdistance her friend
at any time—although she chose not to.

As the two friends swung back toward the Great
Temple on the last kilometer of their run, a third young
woman joined them. Anja, looking rested and relaxed,
had clearly not been out doing calisthenics this morning. But that did not make the situation any less
irritating when the tanned older girl broke into a sprint
and raced ahead of Tenel Ka and Jaina back to the Great
Temple.

It didn't help matters, either, when Tenel Ka noticed
Jacen watching Anja with amused approval from his
vantage point at the base of the Great Temple. She knew
she shouldn't allow the situation to disturb her, but she
had retreated immediately, making some excuse about
the *Rock Dragon* needing repairs. Jaina and Lowie had
followed her. Jacen, Zekk, and Anja had not.

Jaina had moved the *Rock Dragon* out onto the open
on the landing field, and for the next few hours the
companions had worked in a heavy silence. Unfortunately, the activities they normally found so soothing
had brought no comfort today. Tenel Ka grimaced and
replaced another cyberfuze that was in perfect condition.

To make matters worse, her own normally well-
controlled emotions were playing strange tricks on her.
For the past several days she'd had a profound feeling
of *missing* Jacen . . . and Zekk, of course. It didn't
make sense. It wasn't as if the two young men were
gone, as Lowie had been when he'd accompanied his
friend Raaba to visit the Diversity Alliance.

No, Tenel Ka saw Jacen—and Zekk—every day. Yet

somehow, each time she saw the smuggler girl Anja laughing with the two young men, most likely at some joke Jacen had told, Tenel Ka felt an ache that was almost physical.

Perhaps a change of scenery was the answer. If Tenel Ka could get away from Yavin 4 for a while, it might clear her mind—and she might be able to escape the constant reminders that Jacen no longer spent most of his free time with *her*. She found the pain as haunting and indefinable as the phantom pangs she sometimes felt from her severed arm.

Scowling, Tenel Ka touched a probe to a circuit, overloaded it to ten, twenty, thirty percent more than its capacity. The cyberfuze finally failed in a tiny puff of white smoke. Tenel Ka nodded with satisfaction. As she began to replace the component, a loud Wookiee bellow drifted in from outside

"Visitors?" Em Teedee said. "Why, whatever could he mean? We weren't expecting anyone, were we?"

"I do not believe so," Tenel Ka said to the little droid. The whine of repulsor engines filled the air around the *Rock Dragon*. "Perhaps we should investigate."

Jaina yanked the little silver droid's leads free from the navigational control console. "Well, then, what are we waiting for?"

"It's Lando!" Jaina cried. Her spirits lifted even as the *Lady Luck* touched down on the stubbly grass of the landing field not far from the *Rock Dragon*. The sight of Lando Calrissian's space yacht kindled a sense of excitement in her that had been missing for weeks. His visits always meant something interesting.

As usual, her father's old smuggling buddy made a dashing entrance. With a purple cape fluttering behind him, he seemed to glide down the *Lady Luck*'s ramp, his dark, handsome features lit by a dazzling smile. By the time he reached the bottom of the ramp and greeted Jaina and Tenel Ka with a kiss each on the hand, and Lowbacca with a friendly slap between his furry shoulders, Zekk and Jacen were running across the landing field toward them. Master Luke Skywalker followed at a more leisurely pace.

"Hey, what are you doing here?" Jacen asked.

"Are we going to GemDiver Station?" Zekk added. "I've never seen the place, but Jacen and Jaina told me all about it."

Lando laughed. "No, not quite. I'm glad you kids are all here, though, because I have an invitation for you. A business proposal, really."

Jaina exchanged an intrigued glance with Tenel Ka. "We are prepared to assist you," Tenel Ka said. Lowie rumbled his agreement.

Lando grinned. "As it turns out, I already talked to all of your parents and got permission."

"Hey, that's great," Jacen said.

"What is it you need?" Zekk asked.

"Some professional assistance. From professional young people like yourselves. But it's not on GemDiver Station. I've got the corusca-gem mining operation running pretty well by itself. Right now, I'm on my way to Cloud City."

"Bespin?" Jaina said. "You still own property there?"

Lando smiled. "At the moment, quite a lot. You know how I am, always looking for some new way to make credits. I decided I needed to diversify my holdings a bit more, so I talked to one of my old smuggling buddies who lives on Cloud City, and we came up with the perfect investment."

Tenel Ka's eyebrows rose as Lando spoke.

"Old smuggling buddy?" Jaina asked.

"Oh, don't worry, he's completely legit now," Lando said. "He has a wife, two little girls, and all his investments are strictly on the up-and-up."

"What do you need us for?" Zekk asked again.

Lando went on. "Cojahn and I are starting a line of high-tech family entertainment and amusement centers. We're putting the first one right in Cloud City. We're calling it SkyCenter Galleria. Cloud City won't be just for gambling anymore. This place is gonna have rides, restaurants, shopping, the neatest, slickest holomazes, experience chambers, every kind of thrill you can think of.

"I've been interested in this sort of thing for a long time. See, before you kids were even born, I looked into a place called Hologram Funworld as an investment. It didn't work out, but that place was *nothing* compared to what we're building now. SkyCenter Galleria will have something for people of all ages, something for every human or alien in the galaxy."

Luke Skywalker, who had quietly joined them during Lando's description, smiled. "That sounds like one of your best ideas yet, Lando. Do you have some thrill rides that only Jedi can test?" There was a twinkle of amusement in the Jedi Master's eyes.

Lando chuckled. "Not exactly, but close. I was hoping to borrow this fine crew of young people to visit the place with me before I open it to the public. Give me their ideas and opinions, maybe even double check things to make sure there aren't any potential hazards our engineers have overlooked.

"See, my buddy Cojahn has two daughters, a twelve-year-old and a five-year-old, but I need someone a little older to let me know what works for them and what doesn't. These young Jedi Knights could think of it as a vacation, and it'll help me out as well." He winked at Luke. "I promise not to let anyone get kidnapped this time."

The Jedi Master narrowed his eyes thoughtfully and then nodded. "Yes. I think these students could benefit from an opportunity like this."

Lowie gave an exultant bellow.

"Good. We'd love to!" Jaina said.

"We would be honored to assist you." Tenel Ka nodded; her red-gold warrior braids swung around her serious face. "It will be . . . fun."

"Oh, indeed, Master Lando! I should be most gratified if you'd accept my services as well."

Lando gave a small bow. "You bet, Em Teedee. You can never have enough competent droids around on a project like this. I wouldn't think of leaving you behind."

"Hey, speaking of being left behind," Jacen said, "we've got a new friend staying here with us at the Jedi academy. Would you mind if she came along? She's only been here for a few weeks, but she's having kind of a rough time—she's a former smuggler—and I think she could use a change of scenery."

"A former smuggler? Sure, bring her along," Lando said with a bright smile. "She sounds like my kind of young lady."

## ABOUT THE AUTHORS

**KEVIN J. ANDERSON** and his wife, **REBECCA MOESTA**, have been involved in many STAR WARS projects. Together, they are writing the fourteen volumes of the YOUNG JEDI KNIGHTS saga for young adults, as well as creating the JUNIOR JEDI KNIGHTS series for younger readers. Rebecca Moesta also wrote the second trilogy of JUNIOR JEDI KNIGHTS adventures (*Anakin's Quest*, *Vader's Fortress*, and *Kenobi's Blade*).

Kevin J. Anderson is the author of the STAR WARS: JEDI ACADEMY TRILOGY, the novel *Darksaber*, and numerous comic series for Dark Horse comics. He has written many other novels, including three based on *The X-Files* television show. He has edited three STAR WARS anthologies: *Tales from the Mos Eisley Cantina*, in which Rebecca Moesta has a story; *Tales from Jabba's Palace*; and *Tales of the Bounty Hunters*.

For more information about the authors, visit their Web site at
http://www.wordfire.com
or write to AnderZone,
the official Kevin J. Anderson Fan Club, at
P.O. Box 767
Monument, CO 80132-0767